DISCOVERING RACE

TWELVE SHORT STORIES

SIMON LENNON

Discovering Race: Twelve Short Stories
Fiction (Short Stories, Anthology)
Published by Pine Hill Books
ISBN 978-1-925446-34-0 (electronic)
ISBN 978-1-925446-35-7 (paperback)
63,000 words
The characters in this collection of stories are fictitious. Any similarity to
specific real people, alive or dead, is coincidental.
Cover image: Statue of Liberty, her face and eyes shaded, New York, 1998

To my father

CONTENTS

1 EUNICE LEE

Human beings are innately tribal, preferring the company of their own to the presence of others, loyal to their own as their own is loyal to them. Conflicts arise within tribes, but between tribes, tribespeople defend and often advance their own.

So people have unashamedly thought and behaved throughout their histories, whenever their families, clans, and races encountered other families, clans, and races. More often than not, they minimized encounters between races altogether.

With one exception: following the Jewish Holocaust during World War II, the most powerful and influential of European peoples (in Europe and elsewhere) lost interest in their race and races. (Whether there is a single white or European race with different ethnicities or different white races is a matter of nomenclature, as it is for other races and the ethnicities into which they can be bracketed, although other races are much less likely to bracket their race with other races than white people are.)

Those powerful and influential white people (the richest, but not only the richest) ceased advancing their race and decreasingly defended it, but continued advancing and defending their individual selves. Whenever they believed they personally benefited, even if simply by feeling better about themselves, they advanced other races at the expense of their own.

During the ensuing decades, more and more white people meekly followed their leaders into neglecting their race, or spoke as if they did, believing they should. White people who continued caring about their race learnt to keep quiet about it, as they became fewer and fewer.

Two decades into the twenty-first century, when white people mentioned race, it normally wasn't the race of a particular person or group of people. It was the plethora of races coming through the West's porous borders. "Diversity makes us strong," they'd say and repeat. "Immigrants enrich us," they'd say and repeat.

"We are all immigrants, a nation of immigrants," they'd first said in supposedly post-racial America, Canada, Australia, and New Zealand. They increasingly said so in Europe too.

Among them would have been young Eunice Lee, as would have been all the Delawareans she knew in her middle-class neighborhood near Wilmington, except that she rarely gave such matters much attention. If Eunice noticed anything physical about a person, it was his or her hair, because hers was so long, wide, and naturally red. Nobody shied away from mentioning her sprawling red hair, complimenting her for it. So she never shied away from remembering it.

Words she heard said freely about her fiery red hair, she never heard said about other people's black or brown hair, or their hair texture, skin color, facial, nasal or eye structure, or other observable feature of race. Some people wouldn't even mention other people's height, weight, or figures, which also varied with race, at least not in their company (except in relation to children becoming tall or occasionally their adult weight being much improved). They would not mention anything physical about a person, physical differences having been where considerations of race began.

Even beauty was becoming circumspect. Many white people dared not mention it.

Thus Eunice had only her brightly ranging red hair, of note. It made her beautiful, some people implied, although the boys she'd dated more likely said it made her more beautiful. They would.

Whether she really was beautiful, few people Eunice encountered wore hair so noteworthy. That left her with nothing to notice in most people's physical appearance.

If asked, Eunice would have said she only noticed what was inside a person. That was what Americans said, although Eunice never gave any thought about what that might mean. It was probably their character and interests, considered in the kindest conceivable light. It wasn't their intelligence, which was something else Americans didn't like to ponder because pondering a person's intelligence might not be nice, about that person or about others, and because their forebears thought intelligence varied with race.

Twenty-first century Americans said they judged people by the contents of their heart, although they didn't really judge them. Their words merely affirmed their conviction in the innate goodness of people, all people, without evaluating them.

Whatever those phrases meant, Eunice had far more pressing

challenges to deal with. Foremost among them were her college studies and accountancy career looming ahead.

Eunice was among the better students in her accountancy classes at the University of Delaware, although her grades weren't quite enough to get her an internship or interview at any of the major accountancy firms in Wilmington. Since the end of the nineteenth century, Delaware had attracted corporations trading elsewhere with friendly laws, relatively undemanding in terms of cost, compliance, and disclosure. Two decades into the twenty-first century, half of America's publicly traded corporations were incorporated there, even if their only business in the state was paying lawyers, accountants, and other professional advisers.

Smaller than those major accountancy firms in Wilmington, but still a considerable enterprise, was the firm Xiang & Xiang. Eunice's grades had been good enough for the firm to grant her an interview: her first for a professional job, instead of the mere dalliances her part-time and vacation jobs had been.

For that first interview in an accountancy firm and the start of her career beyond it, Eunice cut her long red hair short. Nothing better demonstrated her commitment to her career than cutting her hair; friends and relatives who had stopped mentioning her hair, mentioned their surprise she had cut it. They might have complimented her for her new appearance or might have expressed their disappointment her long hair had been lost, but they never hesitated mentioning it.

As much as her career, her shorter hair demonstrated that Eunice was growing up: maturing into life beyond college, when even college no longer seemed as mature as it once had. Girls wore hair longer than women wore it, and Eunice might have spent too long being a girl; girls in college often did Eunice realized, after she'd finished there. For her interview and coming career, Eunice rehearsed tying her newly short hair in a tight ponytail behind her head.

For that first interview, Eunice bought a dark blouse, jacket, and skirt better than anything else she owned, or had even worn. She bought shining black leather shoes with pointed fronts slight uncomfortable to wear and tall thin heels slightly uneasy with which to step, but she knew her feet and balance would, in time, adjust to them. She also bought a black leather handbag, like the bags older women carried, although not Eunice's unprofessional mother.

To appear what she thought was professional, and to monitor the progress of her journey from home to the interview if not the progress of the interview once it started, Eunice carefully fastened to her wrist a silver watch she'd inherited: the only wristwatch she owned. (She'd never before worn it.) Through her pierced ears, she set her simple silver earrings.

Her new bag in hand, Eunice left home that warm Monday morning not yet used to her new clothes, shoes, or hairstyle, or even to wearing a watch. Always ahead of schedule, determined not to be late to her interview (as she was never late to anything), Eunice arrived early to downtown Wilmington, North Market Street, and finally Hercules Plaza. Loitering outside, intermittently checking her watch, she again rehearsed answers to questions she expected her interviewer to ask.

Eunice had always been good at mathematics, so that accountancy was a logical career. (That was a better answer than saying accountancy offered more certain employment than other professions. It certainly offered better prospects than manufacturing firms like the one that had employed her father, grandfather, and great-grandfather, before her father reluctantly closed it three years earlier.) In five years' time, Eunice hoped to be in a firm like Xiang & Xiang, satisfying the interests of its business clients, solving their problems.

Five minutes before the time scheduled for her interview to begin, eleven o'clock, seemed the right time for Eunice to check her clothes again for any loose fibers or anything else unprofessional. She removed her telephone from her handbag, switched it off, and secreted it back there. She collected her posture, straightening herself even more upright from her new high heel shoes, before bravely joining the adult suits and skirts entering Hercules Plaza.

Inside the building foyer, she checked that the Xiang & Xiang offices were on the floor she already knew they were: the eighth. The directory she'd checked from her home had been correct; the firm hadn't recently moved offices. Before approaching the elevators, Eunice brushed her jacket a final time.

The Xiang & Xiang offices reception area was bright and modern, as she'd expected it to be. No other person waited but, behind the desk and beside the closed door presumably through to the offices, sat a young Chinese woman no older than Eunice. She sat typing at a computer or something else that Eunice couldn't see, looking down in front of her.

Eunice approached her. "Hi," said Eunice. Pausing from her typing, the young woman looked up. "I'm Eunice Lee. I have an interview with Mister Xiang."

"An interview?" the young woman asked. The question didn't startle Eunice as perhaps it should have done. "Do you know with which Mister Xiang?"

"Stanley Xiang," answered Eunice.

"Please sit down."

Eunice turned away. She couldn't help but hear the receptionist behind her speak into whatever telephone or other microphone was at her desk. "I have a Miss Eunice Lee to see Mister Xiang," the receptionist said.

It was the first time Eunice had heard anyone speak her name, her full name, with a title Miss. To hear it in such offices in a downtown office building, Eunice felt she should be there.

In the closest of several wide cushioned chairs standing against a wall, Eunice sat, placing her handbag on the floor beside her. In front of her was a coffee table, on which lay copies of the *Wall Street Journal* and *News Journal*. Reading them might have made a good impression, so Eunice picked up the *News Journal*.

She sat not really reading the newspaper for several long minutes, before the door from the offices opened. Eunice looked up, to see a middle-aged Chinese man dressed in a fine dark suit and tie step through. He looked past Eunice to the empty chairs. He stepped forward and looked around the reception area. Only Eunice and the receptionist were there.

He looked to the receptionist. "Where is Eunice Lee?" he asked her.

The receptionist tilted her head towards Eunice. "That's Eunice Lee."

Taking her handbag back in her hand, Eunice stood up, facing him, but the man again looked to one side of her and then the other, as if a person was hiding behind Eunice and might soon appear. Finally, he looked towards her. "You're Eunice Lee?" he asked.

"I am," she replied, stepping towards him. She thought of offering him her hand to shake, but that would be presumptuous.

"I thought you'd be Chinese, with a name like Lee, a name like Eunice Lee."

"No," she smiled, shaking her head. "I'm American, as we all are." The man and the receptionist both spoke without any accent, or at least no accent different to Eunice's accent.

"Yes, yes, American, I know, but Chinese."

Eunice stood silently. The answers she'd prepared for the interview had not prepared her for this. He'd not actually asked her a question, anyway. "My grandmother's name was Eunice," she explained.

The receptionist sat watching Eunice, as the man did. He had still not introduced himself to Eunice; she only presumed he was Stanley Xiang. "I am sorry for inviting you here," he told her.

"I have Chinese friends," persisted Eunice, "Americans do."

"I'm glad, but I only invited you to come for interview because I saw your name and thought you were Chinese."

"Isn't that illegal?" asked Eunice, certain it was.

"I once invited for interview a man whose family name was Hoy because I thought he was Chinese," the man continued. "He stood where you're standing now and I told him what I've told you. He accepted it."

"I can do all the work you want me to do," Eunice persevered. "I can fit in with everybody; we're all Americans as far I'm concerned."

"Yes, yes," he said, again, "I know we're Americans and I know you can do the work, but you're not Chinese. You should accept that."

"I accept that," answered Eunice, her voice firming up, "but I can't accept being told I can do the work but you won't employ me because I'm white."

"It's not because you're white. It's because you're not Chinese."

"Is that supposed to make me feel better?" asked Eunice. "Wouldn't you be upset if an Indian accountancy firm wouldn't employ you?"

"I wouldn't apply for a job at an Indian accountancy firm. Why did you apply for a job at a Chinese firm?"

"I thought you were an American firm."

"We are an American firm," he assured her, "but you saw the name of the firm: Xiang is a Chinese name. I thought Lee was too, and Hoy, but I was wrong. I accept my mistake. Can we get you a cup of tea before you leave?"

"I don't want a cup of tea," protested Eunice. "I want a job."

"Apply to an American firm," the man told her, "an American firm that isn't a Chinese firm. There are many excellent American accountancy firms in Wilmington, we deal with them all the time, where you can develop your accounting skills and be happy, where you can work hard and become a principal."

"Those firms employ Chinese accountants," said Eunice, certain they did. "Aren't they better because they do?"

"Of course they are," he smiled.

"Why can't you employ me?"

"When you've developed your skills, you might want to establish your own firm. I know Americans like to do that."

"I need to work in a firm now," persisted Eunice. "Are all your clients Chinese?"

"We have many very successful American clients."

"I can help all your clients."

"Please, Eunice, Miss Lee," said the man, before sighing. "Why can't you accept that this is America now? Mister Hoy accepted it. When I told him that I'd presumed from his name he was Chinese and wouldn't have invited him for an interview had I known he was American, he apologized for the misunderstanding. He departed, without causing us trouble. Other Americans respect our wishes to be together without complaining, but not you."

Eunice didn't answer. She didn't know what America was anymore. She didn't know what she accepted.

The man looked back towards the receptionist, as if conveying to her his frustration he could not convey to Eunice. He turned again to Eunice, telling her, "I have tried to be polite, Miss Lee."

"I think you're missing opportunities," Eunice told him, "if you're not willing to employ the best candidates, whatever their heritage."

The elevator doors opened behind her. Eunice turned to see stepping towards her a tall red-haired man dressed in another fine dark suit and tie, carrying a big black briefcase. "Stanley," he greeted the man standing with her.

"Marcus," responded the man Eunice now knew to be Stanley Xiang, moving past her to greet the visitor, taller than he was. "I wasn't expecting you today."

"I'm here to see Mister Xiang. This tax business isn't going away."

Stanley Xiang led the man towards the receptionist. "Have we a room booked for Mister Richmond?" he asked her.

"Room one," answered the receptionist.

Stanley Xiang turned back to the man. "I'll let Mister Xiang know you're here," he told him. "We'll get you a cup of tea." Stanley Xiang went back through the door into the offices.

The receptionist spoke into her microphone. "Green tea in reception," she said.

The visitor stood waiting. He presumably wasn't expecting to wait so long as to bother sitting down.

Eunice knew she should not say anything. She should probably just quietly depart before Stanley Xiang returned, but she'd come too far with too much aspiration (if not expectation) to leave so soon. "Mister Richmond," she said.

He turned around to face her, looking down at her so much shorter than him. He didn't smile. He didn't convey any expression, except waiting for her to speak.

"I'm Eunice Lee," she told him. "I've applied for a job here."

He said nothing, for a moment, as if there ought to have been more reason for Eunice to speak with him than simply her ambition. He might have realized there wasn't such a reason, when he smiled and said, "Good luck."

"Stanley Xiang won't interview me because I'm not Chinese," Eunice told him. "He thought I was Chinese from my name when he invited me here, but he saw me and saw I'm not."

Again, Marcus Richmond said nothing, waiting for more words from Eunice, before speaking. "The only people I've seen work here," he remarked, "have been Chinese."

"Do you think that's fair?" asked Eunice. "Do you think that's legal?"

Marcus Richmond stepped back a little. He looked back towards the door from the offices still closed and the receptionist watching him. He then turned back to Eunice. "Employment decisions," he told her, "are for Mister Xiang."

"You're a client," Eunice told him. "You're an important client; I can see that. I'm sure they'd listen to you. If you wanted them to employ the best candidates for jobs, whatever their heritage, I'm sure they would."

"I am sorry, Ms. ..." he told her. "What was your name?"

"Eunice Lee," she said again. "Don't you in your business employ the best candidates for jobs, whatever their heritage?"

"Of course, I do, but this is not my business."

"Don't you want the best accounting services you can get?"

"I've always been satisfied with Xiang & Xiang. Whatever Mister Xiang does, it works."

The door from the offices opened. Another young woman – Chinese – appeared. Her one hand held the door open and the other carried a small tray, on which stood a small ceramic cup, from which rose some steam.

The door closing behind her, the woman stopped. She looked at Marcus Richmond and at Eunice.

The receptionist spoke up. "The tea is for Mister Richmond," she told her.

The woman carrying the tray took a coaster from the tray, placed it on the corner of the coffee table nearest to Marcus Richmond, and placed the cup on the coaster. (She did so quite deftly, thought Eunice, as if she was well practiced in doing so. Serving tea might have been her only task at the firm.)

Marcus Richmond reached down, picked up his cup with his fingertips around the rim, and sipped from it. The woman returned through that door, back into the offices.

The door from the offices had not yet closed when it pushed open again. Another Chinese man and then another, much older, dressed in suits appeared. They headed towards Marcus Richmond, so much taller than all of them.

"Mister Xiang," said Marcus Richmond, returning his cup to the table. He offered the older man his right hand to shake.

"Mister Richmond," said the older man, shaking his hand, before stepping back. "This is Johnathan Lee," he told him. "I have asked him to join us."

Those three men shook hands, when Eunice also noticed their free hands. On each man's wide wrist was a gold watch conspicuously bigger and brighter than the meagre silver effort on her narrow wrist. The three men then proceeded around a corner, presumably to meeting room one, Marcus Richmond leaving his cup behind.

The receptionist remained at her desk, typing, without looking up. Eunice, the only other person left in the reception area, remained standing. The door to the offices was closed.

Eunice continued to stand. She looked again at the door from the offices hoping it would open. She looked back at the receptionist. "Is Stanley Xiang coming back?" asked Eunice.

"I wouldn't think so," said the receptionist. "Can I telephone for a taxi?"

Eunice couldn't afford to take taxis. Nor could she afford to leave so soon. "Could you please tell him I'm still here," said Eunice.

"I am sure he will contact you if he wants to speak with you again."

"I want to speak with him," insisted Eunice. "The interview hasn't finished. It hasn't even started."

"If Mister Xiang believed the interview wasn't finished," replied the receptionist, "he would have returned. Interviews last as long as the interviewers, not the interviewees, say they last."

Her bag in hand, Eunice stepped towards the door from the offices, causing the receptionist to stand close beside her. Eunice tried to turn the door handle. It didn't turn.

On the wall beside the door was a security panel, with numbered keypads. Eunice pressed the "8" button three times and again tried to turn the handle, but it still didn't turn. She pressed that button four times, but the handle still didn't turn.

"Did you think that would be a Chinese person's choice of code?" asked the receptionist, a little smugly thought Eunice.

Eunice stepped back from the door and the receptionist and turned. She walked towards the corridor along which Marcus Richmond and the other men had gone to their meeting.

"You can't go there," called out the receptionist behind her.

Eunice hurried into the corridor, momentarily slipping from her high heel shoes before collecting herself upright. Slowing a little, she passed the closed door to meeting room one. She passed another open door to an empty meeting room, before approaching the end of the corridor and a closed door.

"Miss Lee!" cried out the receptionist behind her.

Eunice reached the end of the corridor and closed door, where there was no keypad on the wall. Her hand on the door handle, she turned it.

"You can't go there," said the receptionist, close behind her.

Eunice pushed open the door. Ahead of her were several desks at which young Chinese women sat typing, with headphones at their ears and computer screens in front of them. Practically in unison, they looked up at Eunice.

The receptionist stood beside Eunice. "Must I call security?" she asked.

On the inside wall beside them and the open door were several bolts, left unlatched. What the office staff sealed at the end of the working day, they'd left unsealed during it.

Eunice turned back to the young Chinese women at their desks. "Where do I find Stanley Xiang?" she asked.

None of them answered. Beyond them was congestion: more desks with Chinese women sitting at them, along with doors spaced along a wall. Eunice had come far from the relative open space of the distant reception area.

Eunice hurried past those first women at their desks towards the first of the doors, which she pushed open. The room was an office, in which a Chinese woman looked up from her desk. Eunice closed the door.

Behind her, Eunice heard the receptionist addressing someone, not Eunice. "Call security," said the receptionist.

A Chinese man, papers in his hand, looked at Eunice. He stood at a desk, at which a young Chinese woman sat.

Eunice opened another office door. A Chinese man looked up. It wasn't Stanley Xiang.

Closing the door, everybody in sight sat or stood watching Eunice, except for the receptionist. She had hurried ahead of Eunice to an office door several doors ahead. Eunice watched her knock on it, wait, and then enter that office. Eunice started towards that open door, when Stanley Xiang stepped from it.

People who'd been watching Eunice turned back to their work. The man standing at one desk looked back at his papers.

"I came a long way for an interview," Eunice told Stanley Xiang, walking towards him. "I'm dressed for it. I'm prepared for it."

Stanley Xiang looked back at the receptionist, standing beside him. "I will deal with this," he told her.

Eunice reached him. The receptionist left them.

Stanley Xiang looked back through his open door into his office, hesitated, and then stepped back to let Eunice enter. "We can speak in here," he told her.

His office was large, much larger than the other two offices

Eunice had seen. Hanging near her from the wall, beside a Chinese green silk tapestry, was his degree from the University of Delaware.

On the bookshelves behind his desk, there weren't any books. Instead, there were Chinese vases and figurines. In a corner of one shelf, was a small dark statue of the Buddha.

Stanley Xiang closed the door behind them. "Please, sit down," he told Eunice, motioning her to sit in the chair facing his desk.

"Do I get tea?" asked Eunice, sitting down. She placed her handbag on her lap, adjusting herself in her chair.

Stanley Xiang sat in his chair, facing her. "I trust you appreciate this time I'm giving you," he told her. "I don't have to."

"I want Xiang & Xiang to be the best accounting firm it can be," Eunice told him, leaning a little forward in her chair, "by employing the best available people."

"We do employ the best available people, but you've seen most of them now. Is this really where you want to work?"

"Yes," declared Eunice, leaning even more forward towards him and his desk. "I want to be an accountant more than I want to be anything else, and I know your work is very good; Mister Richmond said that."

"Why do you think our work is so good, Miss Lee? Why do you think this office is so cohesive, harmonious, and happy?"

"Are you all Buddhist?" asked Eunice, glancing at the Buddha on the shelves so he would realize the reason for her question. "I like Buddhists."

Stanley Xiang smiled. "No, Miss Lee," he told her, "we're not all Buddhists. Why, we even have Christians here."

"I'm Christian," said Eunice, "sort of."

Stanley Xiang almost laughed. He shook his head.

Eunice looked again around the office: at the shelves and walls, for clues. Surely, the people working there could not have all studied at the University of Delaware. When she couldn't think of anything to say, she looked back at him.

"We are all Chinese, Miss Lee," he explained, as if that alone were an answer. "All our accountants and other employees are Chinese: Han Chinese. We're a Chinese firm."

"We're all Americans."

"I know we're Americans and we like being Americans, but we're Chinese. We work very well together. Why would we lose what we have by employing someone who isn't Chinese?"

"Wouldn't you like diversity?" asked Eunice, repeating what she'd so often heard. "Diversity would make you stronger."

Mister Xiang laughed. "We have diversity," he told her. "We have Americans, Canadians."

"Chinese Americans and Canadians?" checked Eunice.

"Naturally," he confirmed. "We have mainland Chinese and Hong Kong Chinese. Why, the last person I hired was Singaporean Chinese. However clever you may be, Miss Lee, however keen you are to learn and to work, you can't ever learn and work to be Chinese. I wish you every success in your life and career, but you will not be working in this firm. What American firms do is up to them, but what we do is up to us. Isn't that part of being a free country, Miss Lee?"

"That isn't fair."

"What wouldn't be fair would be if we lost our cohesion, became a less happy place to work, because we employed you. I'm thinking of my staff. Can't you?"

"We have laws against racial discrimination, Mister Xiang."

Stanley Xiang shook his head. "Why would you want to work among people who'd prefer you worked somewhere else?" he asked her.

"I just want to work," insisted Eunice. "I won't step in anyone's way; you'll learn to like me. All I'll talk about is work; I won't bring my life outside the office inside it."

"I don't want to talk just about work, Miss Lee. I want to bring my life outside work inside this office. I can't do that with you."

"You can," pleaded Eunice. She looked past him to the artwork, figurines, and Buddha on the shelves. "I love those ornaments."

He laughed. "But you see, Miss Lee," he told her, "they're not just ornaments. They're my life, my family's life, and however much you might like them, and I'm touched that you do, they're not your life. They're not your heritage. They're not your culture. They never will be."

"Aren't you worried that I'll sue you?" asked Eunice. "There's a law firm in this building, I saw its name in the directory: Potter, something."

Again, Stanley Xiang smiled. "There are many lawyers in this building, Miss Lee," he told her. "There are many more lawyers in Wilmington."

"Racial discrimination is illegal."

Stanley Xiang's smiles became longer, when Eunice would have expected them to shorten. "Please understand Eunice, if I may call you Eunice," he told her, "you will never work at this firm. If you want to sue us, or me, then that is your right, but how do you think other firms in Wilmington will respond to your future job applications knowing your reaction to this interview? Will they invite you to sit an interview?"

"They won't discriminate."

"They might not," he said, "but they'll know that if you sued one potential employer for one reason, then you might sue them for another."

Eunice rested back in her chair. The morning would have been easier to bear had she sat the interview and failed to get the job she might have got. It would have been easier to bear had she fluffed the interview and lost a job she should have got, even if Stanley Xiang had abruptly terminated the interview before she'd finished speaking and booted her from the offices. The worst of possibilities was one she'd never considered beforehand: there was never an interview because she never had a chance.

Slowly, Eunice took hold of her handbag and stood up. Stanley Xiang stood with her.

She turned to the closed office door and walked towards it. The handle turned easily.

He followed her through the open door. Around the offices, people worked at their desks without looking up.

Eunice turned towards the door from which she'd come, when Stanley Xiang interrupted. "This way," he said, directing her.

He led her past more desks and people to a door without a bolt inside. The handle turned easily for him, before he pushed it open into the reception area.

Only the receptionist was there. She glanced up from her typing, saw Stanley Xiang and Eunice, and looked back down again. Her fingers never paused from the keyboard.

Stanley Xiang led Eunice through the receptionist area to the elevator, where he pressed the downward button for her. "I do wish you every happiness," he told her. "Some day, I in my firm might have the pleasure of dealing with you in yours."

Some moments, he could seem kind for having accorded her an explanation, for having accorded her any time at all. The elevator doors opened in front of her.

Outside the building again, in the open air of Wilmington, Eunice needed a cup of coffee. She entered the nearest coffee shop.

The barista smiling towards her from behind the counter was Chinese. Another person behind the counter glanced at her and smiled. He too was Chinese. Collecting cups from tables was a waitress, also Chinese. Eunice promptly turned around and left.

2 EUNICE, AGAIN

Typically hidden from strangers, two decades into the twenty-first century, were the white people who preferred the company of their race to the presence of others, as people of other races continued to do. Primarily older white people, they remained loyal to their race as people of other races remained loyal to theirs. Younger white people retaining such preferences and remaining so loyal often did so because of their parents, grandparents, or other relatives, correcting what they'd been told about race, over and over, at school and elsewhere.

Other white people mimicked the prevailing white view. Primarily younger white people, they'd been told, over and over, that racial diversity was a strength or that races weren't real (unable or unwilling to see a contradiction between those two claims).

Through their learning or experiences, some of those other white people came to prefer the company of their race or became loyal to their race (although others offered the same learning or suffering the same experiences were too wedded to their existing beliefs, or too meek or fearful, to change them). Inadvertently and often reluctantly, they became like people of other races remained, having never lost sight of race. Such older white people rediscovered race. Such younger white people, having previously known only what they'd been told, discovered race.

Among those younger white people, to a point, was accounting graduate Eunice Lee, after her aborted job interview at a Chinese accountancy firm in Wilmington, Delaware. However illegal it was to refuse to employ a person because of her race, Eunice knew that refusing to apply for a job because of an employers' race was legal. She might not have known much of the law, and how little of the law was implemented, but she knew that.

With that in mind, Eunice wasn't about to apply again to work at a Chinese accountancy firm. Nor was she about to apply to work at an Indian, Arab, Jewish, or any other accountancy firm except an American one, to the extent she could infer the race of a firm from its name. (Wasting the firm's time with her application and even an interview wasn't her concern. Wasting her time was.) American in this context meant white American, as Eunice had learnt from Xiang & Xiang, after previously being unaware.

Eunice came to wonder how many other white Americans realized that American often meant, in effect, white American. Her parents hadn't known, until she described to them her interview, or not, with Xiang & Xiang. Her white friends hadn't known until she told them of that interview, although her friend Danika Khatri understood. "It's complicated," said Danika, as people said of anything they couldn't politely explain, or wouldn't.

Most accountancy firms in Wilmington were American, it appeared to Eunice from reading their names on a computer screen. The next firm to grant her a job interview was Scottsdale & Parkyn, with offices in the same downtown building, Hercules Plaza, as it turned out, as Xiang & Xiang. Her interview at Scottsdale & Parkyn was scheduled exactly two weeks after her failed visit to Xiang & Xiang, at eleven o'clock Monday morning. (That must have been the time for job interviews, thought Eunice, at least those at accountancy firms in Hercules Plaza.)

For her second attempt at a first accountancy firm interview, Eunice prepared much as she had prepared for her first attempt, but with no need to cut her red hair again or buy what she'd already bought. For the second time, she dressed that Monday morning into her only professional clothes: her new dark blouse, jacket, and skirt. She still struggled a little to slip onto her feet her new shining black leather shoes with pointed fronts. Wearing them, she still found them uncomfortable. Walking in them, she still found those tall thin heels uneasy.

Eunice tied her shortened red hair behind her head, checking in the bathroom mirror that it was all neatly pulled from her forehead and face. She applied just enough make-up to her face to show she had taken the time to apply some, but not too much. She again adorned her ears with her small silver earrings and her wrist with her small silver watch, such as they were.

For all her labors not yet natural to her, Eunice prepared with less anxiety but also less enthusiasm than she prepared the previous time, uncertain there would ever be an interview. She left home later than she'd left home two weeks earlier, carrying her new black handbag. She arrived at Hercules Plaza, along North Market Street, at almost the due time for the interview to start: eleven o'clock, again.

The same elevator Eunice had taken two weeks earlier to the offices of Xiang & Xiang took her to the offices of Scottsdale & Parkyn. Thankfully, the offices of Scottsdale & Parkyn were on a lower floor, so she didn't risk looking out to the offices where she'd been.

On the fourth floor, Eunice stepped out to an offices reception area, as strange and familiar as the one upstairs she'd visited two weeks earlier. All in all, the offices were much the same, although the walls and furniture were different shades of silver blue to those upstairs and a different reception desk and different chairs stood in different places. Between those chairs was a coffee table as there was upstairs, but this table was glass topped as the one upstairs was not.

In a corner of the reception area stood a large white pot, from which rose a deep green plant and leaves. Eunice could not quite decide whether the plant and leaves were real or artificial, as was only a question in downtown city offices. In any other place, she'd presume plants were real.

More importantly, the woman tending to reception, dressed and typing much as the receptionist had dressed and typed at Xiang & Xiang, was white. She was older than the receptionist at Xiang & Xiang and thus older than Eunice, but she was white. Eunice breathed a little easier.

Eunice proceeded to the reception desk, where the receptionist did not look up from her typing and screen. When Eunice had waited long enough, without the receptionist seeming to have noticed her, Eunice spoke. "I'm Eunice Lee," she said.

The receptionist looked up at Eunice. She stopped typing.

"I have an interview with Mister Scottsdale," said Eunice.

"Take a seat," the receptionist told her, with a voice as American as Eunice's (although the receptionist at Xiang & Xiang had also spoken with an American voice). "Someone will be with your shortly."

Eunice took a seat in one of the chairs around the coffee table, her handbag on her lap. On the table were two newspapers and a magazine, but Eunice was not bothered to pretend reading them. Beside them, catching her eye as it was plainly intended to catch people's eyes, was a colorful glossy newsletter. Staring up from it was a large photograph of a smiling clean-shaven black man, wearing a gentle well-fitting suit.

Barely able to help herself, Eunice picked up the newsletter. Scottsdale & Parkyn was delighted to announce the appointment of Malik Freeman to the firm. Like Eunice, he'd studied at the University of Delaware, although Eunice could not recall him. There'd been a lot of students at the University of Delaware. The newsletter was undated.

What Malik Freeman's appointment meant for Eunice's chances of getting a job at the firm, if anything, she didn't know. She returned the newsletter to the table.

Eunice looked around the reception area. Beside the receptionist's desk was a closed door with a security pad sealing it, altogether the same as the door to the offices of Xiang & Xiang.

That closed door opened to reveal a tall man carrying a piece of paper. With a slight wave to his short fair hair, a long moustache, and with command in his step, he too was white. With his race came a sense that Eunice would be judged on her merits.

Having come through the open door, letting it close behind him, the man stopped. He looked around, glanced back to the receptionist again typing, and then looked to Eunice. "Are you Eunice Lee?" he asked, sounding particularly unsure.

Collecting her bag in her hand, she stood up to greet him. "I am," said Eunice.

"I had thought you were Chinese."

Eunice could, there and then, have slumped back down into the chair from which she'd stood, if not the floor below it. Holding her legs fast, she remained standing.

The man began scratching his head. "This is awkward," he said.

It was all much too familiar for Eunice, except that this man was white. She wasn't certain how big a comfort that could be.

He turned back to the receptionist. "Is meeting room one free?" he asked her.

"It is."

He looked back at Eunice. "I'm Walter Scottsdale," he told her, offering her his right hand to shake.

She shook his hand, careful to be firm but not too firm, as her father had advised her to be. "Thank you for seeing me, Mister Scottsdale."

"Follow me," he told her, leading her away from the reception area around a corner to a short corridor. The doors along the corridor were open, and he led Eunice to the first of them. There, he waited by the door for her to enter. When she had entered, he closed the door behind them.

Eunice remained standing. In the room was a large timber table with eight chairs around it. Through a window was a view of city buildings. For that moment at least, she felt she'd embarked upon her career.

Aside from the view, it might have been the most comprehensively bland room in which Eunice had ever stood. The room was blander than even the blandest of university rooms in which she'd studied.

Walter walked to the side of the table near her. "Sit down, Eunice," he said, as he sat in a chair facing her.

She sat in the nearest chair, facing him across a corner of the table. She placed her handbag on the floor beside her.

Walter lay that piece of paper on the table in front of her, but not as if he was about to read it. The paper was a printed copy of Eunice's application to work there.

"I want to be honest with you, Eunice," he told her. "When I saw your name, I assumed you were Chinese. Not just your family name, but I've only met Chinese people of your age with names like Eunice."

"My grandmother's name was Eunice."

Walter nodded. "That explains it," he said. "I think my grandparents also had names I only ever hear now from Chinese. I think they find them in old books."

"I like my name."

"This firm supports diversity," resumed Walter, "and we're trying very hard to increase our representation of minorities. You understand, don't you?"

Eunice sat staring back at him, in her best business attire and with an accountancy degree to her name from the University of Delaware. Within her head was every skill the firm required and a commitment to working hard and well, but none of it mattered as much to her getting a job as did her race. "No," she answered.

"No?"

"No," Eunice repeated. "Doesn't anyone want to hire the best candidate for a job, without regard for race? Two weeks ago, upstairs from here, Xiang & Xiang wouldn't employ me because they only employ Chinese. You won't employ me because I'm white. If immigrant firms don't employ white people in the name of homogeneity and American firms don't employ white people in the name of diversity, where are white people supposed to work?"

"I think Xiang & Xiang is making a mistake."

"You might," said Eunice, "they don't, and they're the ones deciding who they'll employ, not you. What is so good about diversity? It just creates problems."

"Our employees support it."

"Are they missing out on jobs because of it?" asked Eunice. "Are they losing their jobs because of it?"

"They're missing out on promotions because of it."

"Are you missing out?" asked Eunice, without expecting an answer. "If you thought I was Chinese from my name, then so might everyone else. I've got the name you want; I don't need to marry an Asian to get it. You can hire me, put my name in your newsletter without my photograph, and we'll all be happy."

"Please, Eunice," said Walter.

"If you need my photograph for the next newsletter to leave in reception," continued Eunice, sitting forward in her chair, "I could dye my hair black and straighten it. I could inject whatever's in Asian skin to give it that color; I'm probably not allowed to say what that color is. A surgeon could Asian my eyes, cheeks, nose, and the rest of my face. We could take cultural appropriation to a whole new level: racial appropriation, but that's what it seems to take for white people to get jobs in America."

"That isn't necessary."

Eunice sat back in her chair. "So you're interviewing people with Asian names," she said. "How can you tell black applicants?"

"Many African Americans have distinctive names. You should be sensitive to that."

"The ones studying accounting with me didn't, I think," said Eunice, although she'd never really noticed. "You could search social media for photographs or ask job applicants for them? You could have done that before inviting me for interview; some employers do."

"Diversity doesn't mean hiring black people," explained Walter. "Diversity means not hiring white people."

Again, Eunice leant forward in her chair, close to the meeting table edge. "If I forced my way through your security doors into your offices," she said, "would I find a workforce entirely white, apart from Malik Freeman?"

"Who is Malik Freeman?"

Eunice was somewhat surprised she needed to tell him. "Your much vaunted employee," she answered. "I read your newsletter."

"Our newsletter?" asked Walter. "Oh, yes."

Eunice took the time to think, before asking: "How old is that newsletter lying for all to see in the reception area?"

Walter withdrew a little in his chair. "That was someone else's idea," he said.

"There was no date on the newsletter," persisted Eunice. "I checked. How many years has it lain there, while newspapers and magazines come and go?"

"None of our clients objects."

"Do they come to your reception area often enough to know it's the same newsletter and same man pictured there," asked Eunice, "or do they not remember from one visit to the next? As long as he's black, or not white, they forget the rest?"

Walter withdrew a little more. "You're the first person," he said, "I remember mentioning our newsletter."

Eunice sat back in her chair. "Without this interview and you telling me you don't hire white people," she said, "I wouldn't have mentioned it."

"I might have made a mistake inviting you here," admitted Walter, strangely defensively for a job interview he granted her. In their chairs facing each other across their corner of the table, Eunice could have forgotten how tall he had been when first she saw him.

In the silence in which they sat, Eunice slowly wondered why he didn't end their interview then. "Do you leave that old newsletter in the reception area," she asked, "so people visiting your offices know you hired a black accountant?"

"I am interviewing you, Eunice. You're treating this as you interviewing me!"

Again, Eunice leant forward in her chair. "Where is Malik Freeman now?" she asked. "If after this interview, I went to the reception desk, or I came back another day and went to the reception desk, and asked to see Malik Freeman, what would the receptionist say? If I found Malik Freeman from Delaware on social media, knowing what he looks like, and contacted him, what would he tell me?"

"He works out of the office."

"Why does he work out of the office?"

Walter in his chair looked down towards the table edge; it must have been comfortably familiar and inanimate, thought Eunice. His finger appeared from beneath the table and began tapping the table edge.

"Do other employees work out of the office?"

"Sometimes," answered Walter, without looking up, his finger continuing to tap. "Wouldn't you like to work out of the office?"

"I studied accounting at the University of Delaware," said Eunice. "Why don't I remember Malik Freeman?"

Walter's finger stopped tapping, as he looked up at Eunice. "Do you remember everyone who studied accounting at the University of Delaware?"

"Why did your newsletter speak of Malik Freeman studying at the University of Delaware without mentioning his qualifications?" persisted Eunice. "Did he graduate? Did he study accounting, or bird watching?"

Walter's finger again tapped the table. He looked back down again.

"You hired him to tell everyone you'd hired him, didn't you?" asked Eunice, although she was really telling him. "You hired him to declare your devotion to diversity, didn't you? Well, has diversity made you stronger, Mister Scottsdale, has it?"

Again, Walter's finger stopped tapping as he looked back at Eunice. He sat up a little in his chair, without towering as he should have. "I could terminate this interview, now," he told her.

"You haven't 'though, have you," said Eunice, again wondering why he hadn't. "I think you're concerned I might complain to others about not being employed here because of my race."

Walter laughed. "Nobody listens to a spoilt white girl complaining she hasn't got something she wanted," he told her.

"I'm not spoilt."

"You're white, you're spoilt," said Walter. "Welcome to diversity."

"I'm female," Eunice remonstrated, as she'd never before felt she needed to point out. "What happened to gender diversity?"

"That's for white people fighting between ourselves," explained Walter. "Don't expect Chinese, Indian, or any other minority men to give way to white women the way white men do."

After taking the time to ponder his words, Eunice nodded, not meaning to agree but meaning to show she had listened. "Chinese, Indians, and other immigrants are doing very well," she told him. "Why aren't they spoilt?"

"You step outside these offices and claim they're spoilt," Walter told her, "and they'll deluge with cries that they're not. They'll complain they're excluded from something somewhere, even where they're doing better than we are. They'll say they've earned their success in spite of us holding them back, and who among us dares deny it?"

"Why don't white people deny we're spoilt?" asked Eunice, in a small sense that she and Walter Scottsdale were on the same side after all. "Why don't we say we've earned our success?"

Walter shook his head. "They'll say you're only proving how spoilt you are," he replied. "That's not only immigrants who'd be telling you that. White people will too, rather than risk immigrants complaining about them."

Eunice continued staring at him, certain there was a reason Walter Scottsdale tolerated her. "If you're not worried about me complaining that you're discriminating against me," she said, "then it's Malik Freeman, isn't it?"

His eyes momentarily left her. They soon returned.

"You're not certain what I'll do with the story of Malik Freeman, are you?" asked Eunice. "You worry that I'll embarrass you by revealing you have diversity of one: that you leave that newsletter there so people think there's a stream of black accountants working here, when the only one you've got is confined elsewhere, and he might not even be an accountant. Does he know accounting? Can he count to ten?"

"He can count to ten," answered Walter, looking down again. "I'm confident of that."

"He's not accounting for you 'though, is he?" said Eunice, without Walter looking at her. "He's not on the other side of that security door from the reception area at a desk and computer terminal like your accountants. He's not stationed at a client's premises where that client can see his worth, although you shouldn't worry about that: your clients are probably so terrified of anyone accusing them of being racist they wouldn't notice anything wrong with him. I'm surprised they and you haven't made Malik

Freeman accountant of the month, month after month, and put that in your newsletter to leave in the reception area. That, you could advertise in the newspapers."

Walter continued looking down. "You presume a lot, Miss Lee," he told her.

Whether Eunice was still trying to get a job at Scottsdale & Parkyn or was just venting her feelings, she didn't know, but both were reasons for her to say everything she'd said. Scottsdale & Parkyn wasn't going to offer her a job if she'd politely left to save Walter from embarrassment. Scottsdale & Parkyn wasn't giving her a job anyway.

Walker looked back at her. "Why do you want to be an accountant, Eunice?" he asked.

It was the first normal interview question he'd asked her, thought Eunice, although she'd never sat a normal interview for an accountancy job to know what normal interview questions were, unless her experiences were normal. Whether Walter's question meant that the meeting had become the job interview she'd previously expected, or the question was a ruse to end the previous discussion without seeming to end it, Eunice didn't know. Her answer would be the same in both events. "I like mathematics," she answered; that seemed more professional than saying math. "I'm interested in business. I like thinking."

"You like thinking?"

Eunice hadn't realized there was anything unusual about thinking. Perhaps thinking had come to be more unusual than she'd appreciated.

"Well, thank you for your time, Eunice," said Walter, standing up.

"Is that all?" asked Eunice, remaining seated.

"We'll be in touch," he smiled, opening the meeting room door.

Eunice remained seated. "Being white," said Eunice, "have I got a chance of getting a job here, or will you now go back to your office and look back at the job applications you've received and the applicant directories to find an Asian name: a solely Asian name, this time? Will you look for photographs of the applicants in social media so you don't get it wrong, or ask the applicants for photographs under the pretext of something other than checking their race? You could say it's for building security; we trust everything in the name of security."

"You have a chance of getting the job, Eunice."

She was uncertain whether to believe him. She didn't believe him.

Again, Walter smiled. "None of us get every job we apply for," he told her.

Eunice collected her bag in her hand and rose from her chair. Having been seated, although not for very long, she stretched her muscles a little, in the discrete manner women did. Walter ushered her from the meeting room, walking behind her back towards the reception area like he was herding her away, ensuring she left.

The receptionist was again typing at her desk. She did not look up.

At the elevator, Walter pressed the downward button, much as Stanley Xiang had done two weeks earlier. "Thank you for coming, Eunice," he smiled, all very ordinarily. "We'll be in touch." Contacting her to tell her she hadn't got the job would be his moment to wish her future success and happiness, as Stanley Xiang had done.

Like Stanley Xiang, Walter remained there, as if he too feared the elevator might come and Eunice might not enter it. When it came, she entered it. Turning around and facing him, she watched the elevator doors close in front of her, his smiling face disappearing as they did.

Downstairs, walking back through the building lobby, Eunice slowed. She had nowhere else to go, but that image from the newsletter remained fresh in her mind. She stopped, turned around, and returned to the elevator.

There she waited, allowing time to ensure that up on the fourth floor, Walter had left his reception area, passing back through that security door to his secret offices. She then entered the elevator.

Again stepping into the offices of Scottsdale & Parkyn, Eunice approached the receptionist at her desk. "Is Malik Freeman in today?" Eunice asked her.

"I haven't seen him," she answered, looking up. "Do you know him?"

"We were both at the University of Delaware," explained Eunice. "I'd love to see him."

"He does deliveries."

"Deliveries?" checked Eunice.

"If you leave me your number," said the receptionist, "I can ask him to call you."

Eunice smiled. "I shouldn't impose," she said. "Thank you."

She again left the offices, boarding the elevator back down. Eunice's knowledge of Malik Freeman probably wouldn't mean anything, but might be fun to mention when Walter told her she wasn't getting a job at Scottsdale & Parkyn. She would say she didn't want a job doing deliveries, anyway.

In the lobby of the Hercules Plaza, wondering what she should do or where she could go, except home, Eunice stopped, among the scores of men and women coming and going past her and around her. She stood dressed in professional clothes as every bit as good as theirs, she felt, as she was every bit as good as they were, except that they were employed, probably, but she was not. One or two men or women were dressed casually, but they were still dressed better than most people outside. They moved with all the purpose that others there moved, as employed people did.

After two job interviews, or two attempted job interviews, for which her foreign-seeming name introduced her but her race excluded her, Eunice could hardly help but notice people's race. She'd learnt that everybody else noticed, in spite of her having been told at school and college that they didn't, so she might as well notice too.

Those men and women streaming around her were primarily American, but there were Asians in greater proportion of the total than in most of Wilmington. Conversely, there were fewer African Americans.

Among those African Americans headed towards her was one curiously familiar. He wore a suit, although not the finest suit around her and not the suit she had previously seen him wearing. She hadn't met him, but she'd seen him in a photograph, in an accountancy firm newsletter. Much shorter than she would have guessed from that photograph, without any reason she should have guessed he was tall, he was not much taller than she was.

Eunice stepped in his way. "You're Malik Freeman," she said, as much as a statement to someone who hardly needed to be told as a question.

He stopped in front of her. The people walking behind him walked around him and Eunice. "Do I know you?" he asked her.

"I've just been in the offices of Scottsdale & Parkyn," she explained. "I saw your name and photograph in the newsletter."

He laughed. "I told my mother people look at that," he answered. "She'll be so proud."

"Why are you doing deliveries?" asked Eunice.

Malik stepped back from her. "It's good money," he replied, "and won't turf me in jail."

"But you studied at the University of Delaware. What we're you studying?"

"To be honest," said Malik, "I can't remember what I was supposed to be studying, the course I was enrolled in, but I played a lot of football, went to a lot of parties, and had a lot of good living."

"Wasn't that a waste of your tuition fees?"

"I was on a scholarship."

Eunice nodded, with her ever unfolding realization. "I would have liked a scholarship," she said.

"Mine didn't do me any good. It did the donors good because someone told me it did them good, but it didn't do me any good."

"Does it bother you when white people use you to boast about diversity?" asked Eunice.

"I can always refuse them."

"I can't," said Eunice.

Malik shrugged his shoulders, before looking past her towards the elevators. "I should go," he told her. "I might have more deliveries to make."

"You could make quite a life from white people's love for diversity," persisted Eunice.

Malik smiled, looking back at her. "I could, couldn't I?"

Eunice laughed. "You deliver those letters and parcels without any problems," she told him, "or without too many problems, Scottsdale & Parkyn might put you in charge. The firm might become Scottsdale and Freeman, or just Freeman's, with pictures of you not just on old newsletters, but on all the walls."

Malik laughed. "Why not," he asked, looking wistfully away, "why not?"

"Why not, indeed?" asked Eunice, not so wistfully.

As his wistfulness faded from his face, Malik turned back to Eunice. "My parents told me white people love black people," he explained, his smile leaving his face altogether, "but only when we look nice. White boys can do what they like, but I've got to shave my face every day, keep my hair short, and never wear jeans or a hood. If I don't, people get scared. Even some black people get scared."

Eunice's smile had also left her. "I'm wondering why I ever studied," she told him. "I wonder why I bothered."

Malik continued looking at her. He plainly didn't understand, but he hadn't studied as Eunice studied.

Appearing beside them was Walter Scottsdale, his moustache catching Eunice's attention more than it previously had. "I didn't expect to find you two together," said Walter. "I was on my way to a meeting when I noticed you both."

"I know about Malik making deliveries," Eunice told him. She might as well have told him.

"Malik needs a job more than you do," replied Walter.

"Why does Malik need a job more than I do?" she badgered him.

"Do you want to do deliveries?"

She dipped her head. "No," she admitted, although with her University of Delaware degree she felt she needn't admit anything. She looked back up again.

Walter turned to Malik. "Haven't you deliveries to do, Malik?"

"I'll see," said Malik, leaving them.

Eunice remained with Walter in the lobby of the Hercules Plaza, among the working men and women bustling around them. "Will you be interviewing all our employees?" Walter asked Eunice.

"I recognized him from your newsletter."

Walter scratched his head. "I will have to research job applicants before interviewing them," he admitted. "I'll contact you when I've decided what to do about the accountancy job."

"And wish me all the best for my future, with every happiness?"

Walter smiled. "Yes," he told her, as he walked away through the lobby and out of the building.

Eunice slowly followed him, only because she might as well follow him. In the open air again, her bag in hand looking much like a person working, she trudged slowly back towards the railway station.

Near the railway station, a black man looking the worse for wear sat on the edge of the sidewalk, with an upturned cap in his hand begging for money. Other Americans gave beggars loose coins from their purses or wallets, without making eye contact with them, but Eunice approaching this beggar made eye contact. She smiled at him.

The beggar's eyes stayed with hers. His hand raised his cap higher, inviting her generosity.

Still smiling, Eunice shook her head, politely declining him as she continued walking towards the railway station. If he'd been white, she'd have given him money.

3 CHARITY

Being convinced as they were of the goodness of other races, white people never saw themselves as the most charitable people on earth. They only compared their charity with each other, and if the people of Massachusetts weren't the most charitable of Americans, they certainly felt they were.

Never comparing himself to others, except to feel the responsibilities of his privileged upbringing, was young Aidan Grant. With his neat blond hair carefully parted and a scholar's large round thin-rimmed spectacles, along with his woolen vests when the air was cool but not so cold as to warrant a woolen jumper or coat, the Bostonian looked every bit the school leader he'd been. Even at college, his face appeared more like it had never needed shaving than one closely shaved each morning.

For as long as he could recall, Aidan's family had sponsored poor children in Africa, sending money for them every month. He and his family were parishioners at the historic Old South Church along Boylston Street, to whose bank account the family sent monthly offertories, including ten percent of Aidan's weekly allowance from his parents. There was thus nothing more natural for Aidan to do of Saturdays he wasn't studying than visit sick and elderly parishioners in their homes, keeping their gardens and otherwise helping them when they were less able to help themselves.

Aidan was a fine young man everybody said, not just his girlfriends. With excellent grades from an excellent college and all the right subjects and major to study law, as well as impressive referees, Aidan applied to study law at Harvard University and other prestigious university law schools confident he would be accepted, but he was refused admission to all of them. The reasons for their refusals he didn't know, but he trusted God and America that they were right.

Thus Aidan volunteered to help at the church and elsewhere, while he considered what else to do. Succeeding his father in his family's printing business was one option, although his father was in no hurry to retire and his busy mother was in no hurry for his father to retire. Living in his lavish family home, with an increased allowance from his parents since he'd graduated from college, Aidan had time to contemplate.

Aidan also had time to conceive and organize a Christmas stall. Poor parents would need only to come to the stall after noon on Christmas Eve to receive a gift for them to take home and give to each of their young children Christmas morning.

In the weeks leading up to Christmas, the church advertised Aidan's coming Christmas stall to its congregation and outside. Reflecting the ethos of the church (although not its heritage), the church called the stall a holiday stall.

Aidan collected colorfully wrapped presents from friends and parishioners, as well as buying some he then wrapped, until he must have collected more than a hundred gifts. The morning of Christmas Eve, he brought them all from storage at his home and in the church to a space set aside for the purpose inside the church doors. On tables set there, he laid out those gifts to make them easy to choose, although people could have no better idea than Aidan had what was inside the wrapping. When the gifts spread out became too numerous to fit on the tables, he placed them in small piles.

Some presents were big, others small. Some were flat, others tall. Some were cubic or rectangular and others spherical; the spherical ones were relatively easy to guess.

Wandering near Aidan and his stall every so often, not really to oversee him but to express her support for his enterprise, was the church's Senior Minister and Chief Executive Officer, Heloise Fowld. (When everything else in America had become a business, churches had too. Churches formalized the chief executive function of their senior ministers, more so than any ministerial function of their chief executives.) Heloise's soft complexion and gentle manner in conversation belied the officiousness with which she administered the church.

Heloise smiled at Aidan, as she normally smiled at people. She was always pleased with her parishioners, as she was not so pleased railing against America's political leaders outside.

Aidan affixed a notice to the front of each table repeating the instructions previously advised: the gifts were suitable for young children, provided free to parents too poor to buy them, one gift per child. Outside, the church noticeboard informed passers-by that the holiday stall commenced at noon. Everyone was welcome.

The weather was particularly cold, without snowing. Only great need and love for their children would bring people through the streets of Boston to the church, thought Aidan.

The church was open for more than just the stall, so that the first people Aidan saw entering the church were parishioners, smiling to see Aidan standing before those gifts. "You have done well," said one parishioner, before proceeding into the church.

Aidan couldn't imagine any of the church families he knew needing charity, although parishioners were no less welcome to take gifts than was anyone else if they needed them. None did.

The first stranger to enter the church and stop at the stall did so before noon, but Aidan was well set up so being early didn't trouble him. He stood there tending to her, sometimes stepping along behind his table towards the second person browsing. Aidan was ready to answer people seeking help, without knowing what help they might want.

One woman dressed poorly examined several gifts, before taking two that she placed in her small fishnet bag. "Thank you," she said to Aidan.

"Merry Christmas," he replied.

"Merry Christmas," she said, and departed. Other men and women took one, two, or maybe three gifts each.

Aidan recognized the church's parishioners for being better dressed than other people were, with hair better groomed and skin better kept, but one woman examining the gifts appeared dressed a little too well to be poor. She made Aidan realize he had no provision for checking whether a person was poor. He could hardly ask for proof of poverty, in the form of food stamps or the like, but what charity could check such entitlement? Aidan could only trust people taking gifts that they needed charity.

Dressed decidedly better than other people there, including many parishioners, was a man about thirty years of age, wearing a new suit less fashionable than others Aidan had seen but a new suit nevertheless. Around his whiskered face was a black beard unusual enough in Massachusetts, but he wore it without a moustache or other hair near his mouth.

His skin was pale but harsh, Caucasian but not European.

Immigrants were a particular focus for the church's tireless declarations of inclusion, although Aidan had never seen any like this one in church. Aidan wondered whether his presence implied anything about the stall's appeal, or about the poor people outside their homes on so wintery a Christmas Eve.

Examining the gifts, the man looked at Aidan. "Which presents are for boys and which are for girls?" he asked, with a slight guttural accent.

"We don't discriminate," smiled Aidan. Again reflecting the ethos of the church, although not its heritage, there was no distinction between presents for boys and those for girls. If any donors had distinguished them in their wrapping, they'd not mentioned it to Aidan.

"How do we choose presents for our sons?" asked the man.

"Won't your sons be happy to receive any gifts?" asked Aidan. "None of us know what children want to play with."

"I know my sons," said the man, picking up one gift from the table and pulling off the blue wrapping paper.

Initially too surprised to respond, Aidan needed a moment before tentatively speaking up. "Shouldn't you let your sons open the presents on Christmas morning?" he asked.

"We don't believe in Christmas," he answered, discarding the torn paper to reveal a book about animals. "No," he said, dropping the book back on the table.

"That's a nice book," Aidan protested, reaching forward and picking up the book and torn paper. He folded the paper around the book trying to rewrap it, but it still looked like what it was: torn paper around a book.

The man had already picked up a larger present, from which he ripped off its red wrapper. Inside was a box with a clear plastic front, revealing a doll. "Huh," he said, dropping that.

Near the man stood a woman, a white woman, examining the presents without opening them. She didn't react to the man near her, so far as Aidan could see.

The man started for another colorfully wrapped present, before checking himself and taking another. The present he'd left behind was wrapped in paper marked with Christmas stars.

"Can I help you choose something?" asked Aidan.

"Have you anything suitable for a Chechen boy?"

Aidan stared. He'd have thought anything suitable for one child was suitable for any other. The man departed.

A short time later, Heloise again approached the stall. "So many gifts have gone, Aidan," she smiled. "You will have made some children very happy."

Aidan picked up the discarded book and torn wrapping paper to show Heloise. "A Chechen did this," he told her.

"Let's not dwell upon him being Chechen, shall we?"

Aidan returned the book and paper to the table. He picked up the doll. "He didn't want this for his sons," Aidan told her.

Heloise smiled. "I'm sure he knows best," she said.

Aidan returned the doll to the table. "He doesn't even celebrate Christmas..."

"We can't worry about how he celebrates the holidays," Heloise interrupted.

"Now he's torn open these two gifts," complained Aidan, looking back at them, "other people can't take them."

Never did anything around her seem to faze Heloise. "We can find you some tape to wrap those presents again," she told him.

"The paper is torn."

"We can find you more paper." Heloise left him.

Other men and women came, taking gifts. Aidan slowly realized how few of them thanked him, before chastising himself for having noticed. He hadn't established the Christmas stall to receive gratitude, but because charity was the right thing to do, especially at Christmastime.

Heloise eventually returned with colorful wrapping paper, a pair of scissors, and a roll of adhesive tape. She and Aidan rewrapped the book about animals and the doll, while men and women took other gifts.

Aidan had presumed the poor parents would appear without their children, so that they could surprise them on Christmas morning, but the Chechen returned to the stall with three small boys, dressed as well as any schoolboys dressed. "You find what you want," the Chechen told them, as the boys placed their hands on the presents closest to them. "You take as much as you want."

"No," interjected Aidan, leaning forward against the table edge and reaching his hands across the table to hold down presents the boys touched. The boys pulled back their hands.

"Aidan," interjected Heloise, in an uncommonly disciplinary fashion for her.

"We're offering one gift per child," Aidan told the Chechen, also reminding Heloise.

"We know other Chechens." He looked back at his sons. "Go ahead," he told them. "Take everything we can."

"No," said Aidan again, raising his hands above the presents ready to press down upon any the boys touched.

"Aidan!" snapped Heloise, louder this time. "These are our gifts to the children."

Still leaning against the table and his arms still outstretched, Aidan turned back to Heloise. "These are gifts for poor children," he told her, looking up at her as he did from his stance. "The people who donated them wouldn't want this."

"We're not to judge our donors," said Heloise. "Having donated these gifts to this church, we offer them to these boys."

"One gift per child," said Aidan, "or other children will miss out, while you and I rewrap what these people discard."

"I'm perfectly happy to rewrap the gifts," declared Heloise, "all of them, if I must."

"They're taking advantage of us," protested Aidan.

"I want them to take advantage of us. You should too."

"I don't," said Aidan. "I wanted to help poor children celebrate Christmas, not cater to other people's greed."

"This church shares with everyone," insisted Heloise, "everyone."

It was a sentiment Aidan had heard a thousand times in church, not just from Heloise, without questioning it. He'd doubtlessly expressed it himself, when the prayers or other conversations warranted it, but he'd never before felt those words put to the test as they were being tested that Christmas Eve.

"Aidan?" asked Heloise.

His arms still stretched across the table, Aidan looked back to the Chechens. They stood waiting, more patiently than Aidan would have expected them to wait, but they would have been entitled to think Aidan would soon acquiesce. Indeed, nothing else explained why the Chechens didn't simply spread out beyond Aidan's reach to take presents; he could only ever stop one of them, if that.

Dressed more like the people Aidan had expected to come was a white woman at the table, her dress old and dirty, her hair ragged. She placed her hand on a present beyond Aidan's reach.

"That is ours," the Chechen father told her, stepping across and taking that present in his hand.

"There are other gifts," Aidan told him.

"She can take hers when we're finished."

Aidan glanced at the woman's empty hands. "She hasn't taken any gifts," he told the Chechen father. "You're trying to take them all!"

"Aidan!" snapped Heloise.

"These boys are already happy," replied Aidan, without looking at Heloise, "but a gift might make this woman's child happy."

Heloise was unperturbed. "If we run out of these gifts," she told Aidan, "we can get more."

"This is Christmas Eve," said Aidan. "We're not getting more donations."

"I can find gifts in the church," said Heloise. "I can buy gifts from the stores."

Aidan again looked back at Heloise. "When do we stop giving?" he asked her.

"We don't."

"I'm ready to stop."

"Have you ever recognized the good we do by giving," asked Heloise, "until we have no more to give?"

"There's no good in giving," Aidan corrected her, "to people who will only ever take."

"How many people find glory because we give?" asked Heloise.

"None," answered Aidan, "not like this."

The Chechen father interjected, although the conversation was really about him anyway. "You're only speaking like this," he told Aidan, "because we're Chechen."

Aidan again looked back at him. "I'm speaking like this," replied Aidan, "because you're trying to take everything."

"Why shouldn't we take everything?"

"What do you ever give poor Americans?" Aidan asked him.

"Aidan!" Heloise scolded him. "Let us do the giving."

The Chechen father again spoke. "We have our people to help," he told Aidan.

"So do we," said Aidan, before pointing his head to the white woman still standing there. "This one wants a gift for her child you won't let her take."

The Chechen father looked at the woman. "Would you deny my

boys presents," he asked her, "at Christmas?"

Aidan interjected. "You don't celebrate Christmas," he told him, for the woman to hear.

The Chechen father continued looking at the woman. "You do," he told her.

The woman looked back at Aidan, presumably wanting guidance from him. Aidan didn't speak; he'd said enough.

She then looked at Heloise, who obliged. "There is beautiful religion in Chechnya," said Heloise.

The woman looked back at Aidan and then the Chechen father. "I'm sorry," she said, although Aidan couldn't imagine the reason for her apology or to whom it was directed. It might have been directed at all of them. Without having taken a thing, she turned and left the stall and church.

"Boys," said the Chechen, "you pick your presents now."

"No!" again cried Aidan, leaning even more against the table and his arms stretching out further, his floating hands again ready to pounce upon gifts the Chechens tried to take. "Other parents will come."

"Aidan!" again scolded Heloise.

"What kind of a church are you?" the Chechen asked Aidan.

"I'm trying to decide."

Heloise answered for him. "We're a giving church," she told Aidan, more than she seemed to tell the Chechens.

Still leaning against the table, his arms outstretched, Aidan looked back at her. "We're a church," he answered her, "with people to help, but not for people to exploit."

Heloise persisted. "We *are* a church for people to exploit," she corrected him. "Have you forgotten Jesus' example?"

"Jesus was no patsy," Aidan corrected her, "but we're patsies: helping people who don't need our help instead of people who do, giving everything to people who think even less of us than they already did because we do."

Heloise shook her head. "I never thought I'd hear in this church such evil…"

"I'm not speaking evil."

"What would your parents say?" asked Heloise. "They would be mortified."

"They and I can talk about that when I see them."

Heloise, as much like a scolding parent as a scolding teacher, glared at Aidan. "I never thought I would say this to anyone," she told him, "but Aidan, I might have to ask you to leave this church."

In a church that proudly welcomed everyone, including people not Christian and even antagonistic towards Christianity, her statement stunned Aidan. The church in which Aidan had sat all his life was contemplating expelling him, to keep welcome a stranger and his sons abusing Christian charity.

Placing her hands on her hips in the most disciplinary of manners, Heloise continued staring down at Aidan. "Our guests can take whatever they take and leave whatever they leave," she told him, "without you or me intruding upon them."

"This is our church," Aidan told her.

"This is everyone's church."

"Then it's no one's church," answered Aidan. "I'll be here tomorrow. That woman who left without a gift might have come here tomorrow. No Chechens will come here."

"That's not important," insisted Heloise. "This church is not important. You and I are not important, but our love and generosity are important."

"This church *is* important," Aidan corrected her. "You and I *are* important."

"Enough," snapped Heloise. "This is not your church, Aidan, and these gifts came to this church to dispense. Step back from the table."

"What about poor children?"

"Aidan!"

Aidan stood still, silenced as much by Heloise's manner as by her words. Slowly, he pulled his hands and arms back, standing upright again. He stepped away from the table, becoming an observer to Heloise and her guests.

Heloise looked to the Chechens. "Please," she smiled, holding out her open hands and arms like Christ at the Last Supper, but not to His followers. "What is ours," she told them, "is yours."

The three boys lunged at the table, pulling open gift after gift, dumping torn paper after torn paper on the floor, piling the opened gifts on each other. There was no obvious attempt to distinguish one gift from another.

From his place away from the table, Aidan watched. "How many can you take?" he asked.

"All that they need," answered Heloise.

39

"They don't need all that."

"Their needs aren't for us to judge."

The Chechen father unwrapped gifts slower than his sons. Among the gifts he opened was a doll. He piled it with the others they seemed ready to take.

"You said you didn't want dolls," protested Aidan.

"Another Chechen might," the Chechen father replied. Another gift he opened again was the book he'd rejected earlier. He piled it with their others to take.

"You said you didn't want that book," protested Aidan.

"We can sell it."

The church door opened. Entering the church was a young black woman carrying a small baby. Their clothes were as dirty as any Aidan had seen that day. Their hair can't have been cleaned or even brushed for days.

The Chechen father turned towards the woman. "You'll have to come back later," he told her.

Aidan interjected. "This is everyone's church," he told the Chechen.

The Chechen father stepped away from the stall towards the woman with her baby. "Wait outside until we're finished," he told her, holding up his arm to usher her and her baby both back to the cold.

Aidan turned to Heloise. "He can't do that," said Aidan.

"You worry about your words today."

The woman and her baby went back outside. The Chechen closed the door after them.

"Can't we help them?" Aidan asked Heloise.

"You stay there," Heloise told Aidan. She stepped away from him towards the closed door, where the Chechen father was tampering with the door handle, trying to lock it. "May I please?" Heloise asked him.

The Chechen father stepped back. Heloise opened the door and went outside. The Chechen closed the door after her. This time, he realized the means to seal it.

Only Aidan remained at the stall, watching the Chechens open gifts, dump torn paper on the floor, and pile those gifts. They could have taken all the gifts still wrapped, but there were presumably some gifts they'd refuse to take: a Bible, perhaps?

Inside the church remained a handful of parishioners, praying and simply being there. Church staff might have been in their offices; Aidan didn't know.

When the Chechens finished unwrapping every gift, with the floor cloaked in wrapping paper like it was colorful Christmas snow, the Chechens stepped back from their bounty. "We need your help carrying this to my car," the Chechen father told Aidan.

"You have a car?"

"Would you deny me a car?"

"I'm not helping you loot my church."

The Chechen father looked around him, as his sons collected all the opened gifts they could in their arms, with no more attempt to select some over others than they'd exhibited throughout their time there together, but still couldn't carry them all. The Chechen father returned to the closed church door, took a moment with the lock and handle, and opened it.

Standing there was Heloise. Her face was crimson, while hints of sleet landed on her shoulders. She could have walked around the church to another entrance, but hadn't.

"We need a trolley," the Chechen father told her.

"We have a trolley."

As if that was her price for readmission, the Chechen stepped back and let Heloise enter. She came through the open door, which he closed behind her. Without obviously noticing the opened gifts on the table or in the Chechen boys' arms, Heloise continued through the church, stepping around the papers on the floor.

The church door again opened. A white man appeared, dressed poorly but warmly.

The Chechen father turned to him. "The stall is over," he told him.

"I'm sorry," said the man, stepping back and closing the door again.

Heloise returned, pushing a trolley on which stood three boxes. Removing the uppermost two empty boxes, she helped the Chechens stuff their gifts into the lowest box, lying on the trolley. Aidan stood watching. "Can't you help, Aidan?" asked Heloise.

"I've helped them enough."

The first box filled, Heloise covered it with a lid, on which she placed a second box. "You can't help people enough," she told Aidan, packing more gifts.

"I can," answered Aidan. "They've only helped themselves."

"You're such a disappointment," said Heloise. "Haven't I taught you anything?"

"I've learnt more today than I've learnt in church for years."

When the third box was filled and the last of the gifts placed on the uppermost lid, Heloise wheeled the trolley towards the door. "Could you please open the door?" she asked the Chechen father.

He did. Why wouldn't he, thought Aidan?

"Thank you kindly," said Heloise, pushing the trolley through the door.

Aidan grabbed his warm jacket and followed them. The Chechens had never removed their warm clothes. Heloise didn't seem to need anything warmer than she wore inside the church.

Outside, few people walked through the cold and slivers of sleet. Those that did wore thick clothes and hats.

The Chechen father led Heloise pushing the trolley, rattling a little on the rough ground. The boys walked beside her, watching the gifts piled high. One small box, containing a remote-controlled toy car, slipped from the top lid and fell to the ground. A Chechen boy picked up the small box and carried it.

Aidan walked behind them, wondering whether he should offer to help Heloise, not the Chechens, by pushing the trolley through the sleet, but she was undertaking that chore because she'd insisted upon letting the Chechens take so much. Furthermore, she'd got the trolley. Besides, the Chechens hadn't offered to push it. She could push it, thought Aidan. She might learn something.

Walking a little quicker, Aidan strode up beside the Chechen father. "Do you have a name?" asked Aidan.

Heloise interjected, "Aidan," she said, "asking people their names can sound intimidating."

Aidan slowed a little, no longer walking with him. He no longer walked with anyone.

Without speaking, the boys walked with Heloise pushing the trolley, one of them still carrying the small box he'd picked up. Their eyes remained trained on the boxes and other gifts piled on that trolley. Nothing again fell.

The Chechen father stopped at a shining black Buick. The car was old, but was still a Buick: a car better than some on the streets of Boston.

"That's your car?" asked Aidan.

It seemed none of them paid attention to Aidan if they didn't have to. They didn't have to then.

The Chechen father opened the trunk of his car. It was empty, prepared perhaps to accommodate so much, thought Aidan.

The boy who'd picked up that small box placed it to one side in the trunk, before stepping back. He, his father, and his brothers watched Heloise load the rest of the gifts from atop the large boxes into their car. She then lifted the uppermost large box from the trolley into the trunk.

Again, Aidan wondered whether to help her. That none of the Chechens helped her and she didn't seem to care might have been a reason to help her. It might have also been reason to leave her in the purgatory to which she'd condemned herself, and in which she seemed comfortable.

"Careful," the Chechen father snapped at Heloise, laying the last large box in the trunk.

"I am so sorry," she said, adjusting that box beside another. The church trolley was empty.

Heloise stepped back from the car, pulling the trolley with her. The Chechen father opened his driver's door, as his three sons opened their doors.

"Happy holidays," called out Heloise.

They didn't answer, as the four car doors closed. The car drove away.

Only Aidan and Heloise remained at the curb. "Aren't you cold?" asked Aidan. The sleet had paused.

"There are people with less to wear than I have," answered Heloise, pulling her empty trolley back in motion. She turned it, and started to push it, again rattling on the rough ground, towards the church.

Aidan spoke, as they walked together. "I would have liked to help those other people who came looking for gifts for their children," he told her.

"I get a special pleasure from helping immigrants and refugees," responded Heloise. "I think we all do."

"I don't," replied Aidan, "not anymore."

"You won't want people misunderstanding you."

"Don't you think they've come to expect our generosity?"

"I hope they expect it," said Heloise. "We should feel humbled if they have."

"I'm not sure I like feeling this humble."

Heloise laughed. "You will," she said.

They soon returned to the church, where a white woman dressed poorly stood outside the door. "I am sorry," Heloise told her, stopping in front her, standing her trolley upright. "All the presents have gone."

The woman's face fell a little forward, as she nodded. "Thank you anyway for conducting the stall," she whispered. "It was a lovely gesture."

Aidan responded. "Chechens took everything," he told her.

"Aidan," Heloise rebuked him.

"I wish we'd kept presents for your children," Aidan told the woman.

"Aidan," Heloise chastised him again, "these matters aren't within our control."

"They are within our control," Aidan insisted. "Simply because we abrogate our control doesn't mean we never had it."

"Your family has been among our most generous," Heloise told him. "You have been among our most generous."

"I'm still generous," said Aidan," but not with everyone, not anymore."

"If you're not generous with everyone," preached Heloise, "then you're not generous with anyone."

"That isn't true," Aidan corrected her. He took his wallet from his trousers, from which he pulled a fifty-dollar bill he gave to the woman. "This is for you to buy gifts for your children," he told her.

The woman looked at the bill without taking it. "That is a lot of money," she whispered. "You're a young man."

"I can afford it," answered Aidan. "I'm cutting back my other giving to help people like you. I'm stopping sending money to other countries."

"I don't want to keep you from sending money," replied the woman.

"Whether you take this money," replied Aidan, "I'm not sending any more money to other countries. I'm only giving money to people deserving of my charity, who won't take advantage of it: people like you."

The woman continued to stare at him. Heloise stood uncharacteristically silently. Slowly, the woman smiled, before reaching out her hand and taking the money. "Thank you," she smiled. "I will come back to church, when I can, when my children are older. To both of you, Merry Christmas."

"Merry Christmas," said Aidan.

"Happy holidays," said Heloise.

"Thank you again," the woman smiled once more. She turned and trekked slowly away.

When she'd gone far enough from them not to be heard, Heloise looked to Aidan. "I know you didn't mean what you said about only helping people like her," she told him. "It was a clever way to convince her to take your money."

Aidan looked back at Heloise, wondering whether to tell her the truth, before opening the church door. "Shall we get you out of the cold?" he asked, taking the trolley from her and stepping back for her to enter the church ahead of him. He pushed the trolley into the church after her.

The stall tables were derelict, still with their notices affixed to them offering toys, books, and other items suitable for young children, one per child, provided free to anyone too poor to buy them. Filling the floor in front of them remained the mass of torn wrapping paper, making the whole church feel derelict.

Heloise took the trolley back to whatever place she'd brought it from earlier. She soon returned without the trolley, but with an empty cardboard box she placed on the floor. With her hand against the table for balance, she carefully knelt down to the floor, where she began collecting torn wrapping paper into the box.

With Heloise appearing then as poor and helpless as any woman who'd come for the Christmas stall that day, Aidan knelt down beside her. He too began collecting torn wrapping paper into the box.

"Thank you," said Heloise.

"Will we see those Chechens again?" Aidan asked her as they cleaned, kneeling on the floor.

"We will have the holiday stall again next year."

"Not with me," answered Aidan, collecting more torn papers.

"Why ever not?" asked Heloise, placing more torn papers in the box. "This year's stall was such a success."

4 ADOPTION

Never thinking about the nature of families was office secretary Tippy Norton, even when her much older boyfriend (probably better called a gentleman friend) businessman Hywell Oakland first mentioned marriage. They were again eating dinner at Ray's Boathouse, watching the sunset warm the wide waters of Puget Sound, Washington.

Draped around Tippy's neck was a light white scarf, as she wore on the warmest of summer days (as warm as Seattle summers ever were). Tippy forever wore scarves and her white scarf seemed to suit whatever dress she wore in Hywell's company; he'd once remarked that he preferred women to wear skirts and dresses than slacks and jeans.

Their conversations often turned to the future, although Hywell talked more of America's future than his; he'd come from a time when Americans did. Even less had they spoken of Tippy's future, which could seem strange given she was more than fifteen years younger than he was and only twenty-three years of age. The future, she felt although never said, would be a much longer stretch for her than for him.

Least of all had Hywell spoken of a future with them together, until that dinner by the water. If sunset was the end of a busy day, it could also be the start of a busy night.

Waiting for their seafood meal, as they always ate at Ray's Boathouse, Hywell studied Tippy's eyes across the table as if waiting for her reaction. "I would like to get married again," he said, in the slow careful manner in which he always spoke with Tippy.

Three years had passed since Hywell's wife died. Four months had passed since Tippy met him, sharing a table with six other supporters of animal conservation, in a huge room filled with such supporters at a dinner in the Hotel Monaco. The name of the venue had let him and then Tippy joke with friends that they'd met in Monaco, when a chance encounter in that exotic European principality sounded a lot more interesting than meeting in a Seattle boutique hotel, even one as nice as the Hotel Monaco.

Through all their lunches, dinners, and excursions together, including one as far away as the Boeing factory, Tippy had often wondered whether Hywell wanted to marry again, but she'd been too afraid that she would seem like she was proposing it by asking. She'd experienced too many relationships that seemed headed to the marriage altar without ever getting there to jinx another relationship by mentioning it but, since Hywell mentioned it, she could mention its logical corollary.

Tippy studied his eyes across the table, waiting for his reaction. "Would you like more children?" she asked him.

Hywell and his wife had been raising their four teenaged children when she suddenly took ill and died. He'd continued the task alone, such of it as remained, with constant advice from his children as to what their late mother would have done in every situation. His family dominated the strangely comprehensive dissertations of their lives that Tippy and Hywell provided each other through that long conversation the first night they'd met, when other diners around the table broke into their own conversations and Tippy and Hywell already knew all they needed to know about animal conservation.

There might have been only two important thoughts in Hywell's head he'd not revealed to Tippy that first evening in the Hotel Monaco. This conversation, waiting for dinner by Puget Sound, would reveal both of them.

"Already having children," answered Hywell, "I can afford to be amiable. I wouldn't want to miss out on marrying the woman I want to marry because of children, so would let my new wife, if I am so fortunate as to get another wife, decide."

Tippy nodded. If Hywell sounded all very reasonable, then it was because he always sounded reasonable, at least with Tippy. "I would like to have children," she said; those thoughts out of her head and expressed aloud to him. "I think everybody, deep inside, does."

"You know," said Hywell, "I will never stop being my children's father. They're the ones who, having met you several times now, knowing everything I've said about you and realizing everything I feel about you and being with you, started telling me I should marry again." Her heart beginning to race, Tippy studied those eyes of his more closely than ever. "They don't want to feel they need to be my companions and I don't want them to feel it, so I brought them altogether at our home last night."

The home remained Hywell's children's home, even though only two of them still lived with him. The other two were at home for the college break. It had seemed a little strange that Hywell hadn't suggested Tippy join them.

"After dinner," continued Hywell, "I gave each of them pieces of paper on which they should write ticks if they wanted me to ask you to marry me, knowing you might refuse me anyway. I asked them to fold the pieces of paper and put them in a small box: their mother's jewelry box, as it was. If just one piece of paper was blank, then I would not ask you to marry me, and there need be no discussion about it."

Tippy felt like a spectator to her life, she'd not been there to see. She didn't know the outcome she wanted, or the outcome that would have led to Hywell telling her about it.

"When we finished," continued Hywell, "I took the box and first piece of paper. Holding it so that only I could read it, I saw a tick."

Tippy relaxed a little, only to feel so liked. She remained uncertain as to the extent she wanted Hywell's children to like her.

"Without telling them, yet, what I had seen," continued Hywell, "I took the second piece of paper, opened it where only I could see it, and saw another tick."

"Phew," said Tippy, smiling at herself, before wondering whether she should have reacted.

Hywell hesitated, before smiling and speaking more quickly afterwards. "I took and read the third piece of paper," he resumed, "and then the fourth, before telling them that all four pieces were marked with ticks."

Like she'd won a beauty contest from the stage of a packed auditorium, Tippy placed her hands to her mouth. Four months could seem so little time to know a man, even one like Hywell she already knew better than anyone else she'd known, including her late parents.

Hywell reached his hands across the table, inviting Tippy to rest her hands against them. "Can I ask you to take on the aggravation of being a stepmother?" he asked her, tears collecting in her eyes where he could not help but see them. "You'd overturn every stereotype there ever was about stepmothers."

She pulled her hands from his and wiped her eyes, as a waiter brought their meals to the table. Hywell pulled his hands back to himself, before the waiter set Tippy's plate on the table before her. He set Hywell's plate before him. Her eyes away from everyone, studying the food before her, Tippy tried to make a decision she had all the time she needed to make. She had days, even months to make it; they had only known each other four months. "Yes," she said.

"Madam?" asked the waiter.

Tippy looked up at Hywell. "Yes," she smiled. "I can take the aggravation."

Their wedding was a beautiful affair, in the church in which Hywell's first wedding was held because that was the only church either of them knew. Needless to say, Tippy didn't wear a scarf.

At their reception up the Space Needle, Hywell and Tippy might have been the only people there not taking time to appreciate the views. Hywell's friends told Tippy what his children told her: that she had made him happy as they'd not seen him since his first wife was alive.

Tippy moved into Hywell's home: another classic hardwood home with views of water and snow-capped mountains, as so many Seattle homes enjoyed, but none of the homes in which Tippy previously lived. Instead of the lesser matrimonial homes her friends had formed, she entered an established family home, with everything in place but hers to change if she wanted to, although the only change she made was affixing a mirror in the hallway near the front door, for her to check her hair and face before leaving the house or before guests arrived.

On her dressing table in their bedroom, Tippy placed a photograph from their wedding and photographs of her late parents and her sister returned to Tennessee. Lying in a drawer, safely out of sight if she hadn't so thoroughly searched every aspect of their bedroom, Tippy found a framed photograph of Hywell with his first wife and their children. His first wife was a pretty woman, but only as Tippy looked long at her did she recognize something of herself, whatever she should make of that. Through all her times in that house, but never in his bedroom until they married and it became her bedroom too, had she seen that photograph.

Tippy showed the picture to Hywell, sitting in an armchair in the lounge room. He sat quietly, looking back at Tippy rather than the face in the photograph he must have already seen so often, before finally speaking. "I didn't think you'd want to see that," he told her.

"I'm not here to replace your past," said Tippy, sitting on the armrest beside him, putting one arm around him and holding the photograph with her other hand in front of them. "I'm here to build upon it."

"But you don't want that picture in our bedroom," said Hywell. "I don't think I want to see that picture in our bedroom, anymore."

"Your children will want to see it," Tippy told him. "They'll want to know I'm not replacing her. I want to know I'm not replacing her."

She thought for a moment about the house she already knew well. Hywell kept a study, but that was private to him and entered by his children less often than Tippy entered it. Besides, she didn't want him alone with anyone but her. Finally, Tippy stood up and took the photograph to their formal dining room, where Hywell's children and other guests often ate. In that most public, least private, corner of their home, she stood the framed photograph on the sideboard.

With her marriage came not just a family home, but supplementary cards to her husband's credit cards. Without the financial insecurities her friends endured, married to men closer to their age and commensurately less rich, Tippy felt assured in her new, carefree existence.

Tippy's stepchildren, like her husband, asked nothing of her. She gave what she wanted to give, did what she wanted to do, while they were happy enough that she was there. Sometimes, Hywell just watched her with a casual, contented smile she only saw because she looked for it, but like she was the only thing worth watching in the room: the only person in the world.

Tippy continued working, in a job that meant even less to her than it previously had. She socialized with her friends and new relations, Hywell's friends and relations becoming hers. Just her and Hywell or with others, they ate in cafes and restaurants whenever Tippy didn't want to cook at home, or eat the food Hywell wasn't very good at cooking, which was most of the time.

Aside from brief visits to Vancouver, which she'd made only to know she'd been to Canada, Tippy had never been outside America before marrying Hywell. They shared vacations into Asia.

Some of the places they visited were hot enough for Tippy to dispense with wearing her scarf, even her thin white scarf she'd packed in her suitcase. Other places warranted her thick woolen winter scarves, and she possessed several of them, wrapped close around her neck. Sometime through that year, she stopped wearing scarves of habit, although she brought them out again for the coldest days.

"Life is easy," she told Hywell, sitting with him in a café on Pioneer Square back home in Seattle, drinking from a glass of Washington chardonnay. They had been married for more than a year. "Thank you."

"Thank you," said Hywell, drinking his glass of the same.

Tippy put down her glass. "I know I said I wanted children," she told him, "but I've been thinking: we already have a family home, we have everything in place, and I've become accustomed to not waiting. I don't want to wait nine months for a baby, and I don't want to get sick and fat, and there are so many people in the world, I'd like us to adopt a baby."

Hywell put his glass down. "I could accept raising our child," he told her, "but I don't want to raise another man's child."

"It will be our child," insisted Tippy. "We'll raise it exactly as you've raised your children; they have all turned out so well."

Hywell continued looking at her, without his usual air of contentment. "Few babies come up for adoption," he pointed out.

"Two days ago," said Tippy, "a woman called me from the church where we married. It seems I mentioned during our wedding preparations that I wanted children and she asked me whether we'd succeeded. The church is persuading women not to terminate their unwanted pregnancies by paying their costs of giving birth and adopting their babies if they still don't want them, which means compiling a list of prospective parents. They have conditions, but from what she said, we satisfy them."

"We're not religious," Hywell reminded her.

"I told her that," answered Tippy, "but she said hers is the kind of church that thinks a loving heart is all that matters in a person, like we do. Some of the mothers insist upon adoptive parents who aren't Christian. She said we'd be a good choice for mothers wanting adoptive parents who aren't religious."

"I would prefer our children."

"Didn't you say you'd let me decide whether we have children?" said Tippy. "These mothers are poor. We could feed a desperate child, clothe it, school it, give it a life so much better than anything else ahead of it."

Hywell again took his glass in his hand, slowly drinking from it, Tippy knew, so he didn't have to speak. Finally, he returned his glass to the table. "What would you want," he asked her, "a boy or a girl?"

"At first," answered Tippy, "all I wanted was a healthy baby, but we shouldn't even think like that. Sick boys and girls need us even more than poor boys and girls do, and we have so much to give them. I would love our child no matter what. Won't our child love us no matter what?"

"The child mightn't love us."

"Your children love you. They love their mother. They love me."

Hywell looked around the café. Tippy knew he was looking for reasons not to adopt a child. The longer he looked around, the harder he was finding it to think of any.

While he looked elsewhere, Tippy spoke. "You were such a good father to four children already," she told him. "We shouldn't waste your talents."

Hywell looked back at her. "Then we can have a child together," he told her.

Tippy shook her head. "This is what I want," she told him. "An adoptive child is no different to a biological child. It's the love that matters, the devotion, and I'll be every bit as devoted to our child that another woman carried for nine months as I would be to one I'd carried. She's simply saving us from waiting, that's all."

"I can wait."

"I don't want to wait," smiled Tippy, confident that her smiles always persuaded him.

Hywell's hand started towards his glass of chardonnay on the table, before veering to the bottle. He poured more wine to fill Tippy's glass and then his own.

Tippy brought her glass near her mouth. "We can keep drinking wine together," she smiled, "while that other mother abstains."

"That other mother mightn't abstain," said Hywell, picking up his glass, "from anything."

"Then that's another reason to think we should raise that child she doesn't want."

With little more to say, but Hywell often looking around the café and Tippy watching him, they finished their bottle of wine. When he looked back at her, Tippy started to stand; Hywell never stood until she did.

They completed the forms, sat an interview, and were awarded a place on a list of prospective parents. Another three months would pass before Tippy was told a baby might become available for them, although there was always a possibility that the mother might change her mind after the baby was born and want to keep it. The father had no interest in the mother anymore and so none in the child.

Tippy showed Hywell the short biographies of the mother and her photograph and of the father without a photograph. The mother was Native American, of a tribe with a name Tippy didn't recognize, as was the father from a different tribe with a name Tippy didn't recognize. (Adoption services recorded people's ethnicity as other American services no longer did. Tippy quietly wished they didn't.)

She looked at Hywell. He looked back at her. Neither one said anything.

Tippy smiled. "This is America," she enthused.

She ceased working outside the home to dedicate herself within it. She bought and read books about parenthood, especially motherhood, and asked her friends and sister for their advice, trying her best to remember all of it. Some of it she imparted to Hywell, although he said he already knew.

"Is it wrong of me?" Tippy asked Hywell, lying together in bed, "but I keep hoping that she won't want her child? I already love it so much!"

The baby, a boy, was born in a good hospital, without any visit allowed from Tippy or Hywell until the mother's time to change her mind had passed. The mother named him Bidziil, meaning strong Tippy was told, but didn't change her mind about offering him for adoption.

Without meeting the mother, at her insistence, Tippy and Hywell adopted Bidziil. He became Bidziil Oakland, collected from the hospital where he'd been born. "Oh, sweetheart," Tippy said to Hywell, cradling their baby in her arms. "I don't think I could have made a more beautiful baby, or given him a more beautiful name."

At their home, Tippy gave Bidziil a room that had already sheltered at least one child to adulthood, with a new cot and baby playthings replacing those that Hywell's late wife long ago gave away. Tippy did everything for Bidziil she felt a mother did: nursing him insofar as she was biologically capable, bathing him, feeding him, and calming him. She held him trying to stand and with his first steps, for as long as he needed her. She read books to him.

As much as they could, Tippy and Hywell gave Bidziil the childhood that Hywell's children enjoyed, with the same care and resources, in all the same places. Where Bidziil's childhood didn't replicate those four past childhoods, it was for more modern technologies making it better.

The youngest of Hywell's adult children moved away. With only Hywell, Tippy, and Bidziil living there, the home came to feel, to Tippy, like it was only theirs.

Hywell's adult children all addressed Bidziil as their brother, although he was two decades their junior and spent much less time with him than they'd spent with each other. There was nevertheless something strange about the evening that Bidziil placed his arm against the arm of one of Hywell's sons. Still very young, Bidziil was about to start kindergarten and elementary school. He and his brother were sitting beside each other at the dining table for dinner Tippy had prepared. They both wore short-sleeved shirts, being Seattle in summer. Daylight remained outside the windows.

From the far side of the table, Tippy stopped eating to watch, her knife and fork resting on her plate. Hywell, seated beside her, continued eating.

Bidziil's brother, Hywell's adult son, left his bare arm against Bidziil's bare arm, for Bidziil's benefit, no doubt. Bidziil's attention conspicuously moved between the skin of his arm and the skin of his brother's arm. His brother, no longer eating, sat still, watching Bidziil.

"I don't want to be different," said Bidziil.

Sitting a little forward in her char, Tippy moved closer to him. "You're not different, darling," she told him.

"I am different!"

The moment was one Tippy had feared, but her response was one she had prepared. "We're all different, Bidziil," she told him.

"I'm especially different."

"We're all especially different."

Bidziil pulled back his arm from his brother's arm. "My skin is different," said Bidziil, standing up from his chair. He left his meal unfinished as he walked from the room.

Leaving Hywell eating and her stepson watching her from the table, Tippy followed Bidziil to the hallway. She found him standing in front of the mirror, with one hand on his hair. He must have been just tall enough to see his reflection there.

"My hair is different," said Bidziil. "It's black."

Tippy stood beside him. "Your hair is beautiful," she told him.

Bidziil's other hand touched his cheek. "My face," he said.

Tippy smiled. "Your face is beautiful," she told him.

Bidziil's hand that had been on his hair touched his nose. "My nose," he said.

Tippy rested her arm behind his head onto his shoulder. Sometimes her baby had come to seem so big, but other times, like then, he remained so small. "Your nose is beautiful," she told him.

With Tippy's arm on his shoulder, Bidziil stood there, staring at his reflection, his fingers pointing at portions of face. He turned his head a little, before placing his hand on his ear.

Bidziil then stepped away, leaving Tippy's arm to fall to her side. Turning back to her, he took her big hand in his small hand. Careful to follow his lead without being a weight or other hindrance, Tippy let him lift her hand. He placed his other small hand beside her big hand.

There, their hands stayed, beside each other. "Do you see, darling?" asked Tippy, watching from above. "We both have fingers, a thumb, and fingernails. Inside, we both have bones and muscles. We're the same."

Bidziil continued staring at their hands. When it seemed he'd seen enough, Tippy raised her other hand. Gently, she took hold of Bidziil's hand not holding her other hand. Slowly, and simultaneously, she turned over both his hands and hers. The palm of his small hand lay open, beside the palm of her big hand.

"From all sides," said Tippy, "we're the same. My hands are bigger than yours, but mine won't grow any more while yours will. Eventually, your hands will be bigger than mine."

Bidziil shook his head. "They're different," he said, pulling his hands back from her. "We're different."

Tippy stepped closer to him and put her arms around his head, pulling him closer to her. "I see only the sameness between us," she said, with all the love and conviction in her.

Bidziil pulled away from her. He walked away.

Tippy took Bidziil to school and collected him afterwards, bringing him home. Other mothers, and some fathers, did the same with their children, in full sight of Bidziil and other children.

One warm afternoon, when Tippy was reclining on a chaise on the lawn behind the house, after the gardener had finished mowing the grass and his other chores, Bidziil approached her. "Why am I different to you and Dad?" he asked her. "Why am I different to my brothers and sisters, to all your other children?"

Tippy sat up from the chaise, pulling her legs over the side so she sat facing Bidziil, almost eye to eye. "Remember, darling," she told him, "see only the sameness."

"No!" snapped Bidziil. "Kids see difference."

Tippy remained sitting there, staring at him. She reached out her arms to him, taking his hands in hers. She tried to pull him slightly towards her, but he leant back, resisting her, remaining in his place.

Ahead of Tippy was the conversation she had often dreaded. For every friend who had advised her to withhold a truth that Tippy agreed was immaterial, another friend advised her to impart what would eventually become self-evident, rather than risk Bidziil learning of it from another source. She might have deferred that conversation with him to Hywell, but that was never really an option; Hywell had refused even to decide whether they should reveal Bidziil's origins to him, leaving all child-raising decisions to Tippy. What followed were the words she had prepared more than any other, but still might be inadequate.

Satisfied his eyes saw only her eyes, Tippy spoke. "Before you were born," she told him, "your brothers and sisters had a different mom to me."

Tippy disliked talk of biological mothers and adoptive mothers for being too clinical and unemotional. They were terms for others to use but not Tippy or her family. For Tippy, there were only mothers; biology mattered less to her than love.

"She was their first mother," she told Bidziil. "I am their second."

Bidziil continued looking at her. Whether he understood her words was less important than him hearing them.

"I'm your second mother, too," Tippy told him.

Bidziil ceased leaning back, resisting Tippy. Her hands holding his hands pulled him a little way towards her, inviting him to speak. "Why does that make me different to you and Dad," asked Bidziil, "to my brothers and sisters?"

If Tippy had thought she could skirt talk of difference, she couldn't. "Your first mother wasn't your brothers and sisters' first mother," Tippy told him. "She was a kind and loving woman," continued Tippy, certain that she was because Bidziil was kind and loving. "She was different to me, your dad, and your brothers and sisters in the same ways that you are different: ways that aren't important, but ways that made her beautiful, and ways that make you beautiful." Her words could sound complicated, even to her.

"Where is she now?"

Tippy smiled; smiles always helped. "She couldn't look after you as we can," Tippy told him. "She wanted you to be happy, so she entrusted you to your dad and me."

Bidziil took time, but slowly began nodding. "Are you anybody's first mother?" he asked her.

"I don't need to be," she smiled. "A mother is a mother."

Bidziil continued looking at her, with all the trust Tippy saw in a child for his mother. Their hands continued holding each other's hands.

Tippy could have left it there, but took the chance to answer a question that Bidziil might never think to ask. "Your father is your second father, too," she told him. "Your first father trusted your first mother, when she entrusted you to us. We call that adoption."

Bidziil remained still, before slowly nodding. Their hands still held each other's hands.

"You're fortunate," smiled Tippy. "You have two mothers and two fathers. Your brothers and sisters only have two mothers and one father. Other boys and girls only have one mother and one father."

Slowly, Bidziil smiled. Tippy wasn't going to be the first of them to release the other's hands but, eventually, he released hers.

Tippy and Bidziil had occasional more conversations like that, insofar as Tippy could have conversations with a child so young, with and without Hywell present. They seemed to be enough, until the afternoon Bidziil approached Tippy sitting in the lounge room, reading a book. "What am I?" he asked her.

Without looking up, she answered, "You're Bidziil Oakland."

"Not who," snapped Bidziil, "what?"

She turned from the book towards him, standing before her. "You're a boy," Tippy told him.

He shook his head. "Not that," he told her. "In this world, what am I?"

"You're an American."

Bidziil shook his head, shoulders, and whole body, as he did when he was angriest. "Not that!" he said again.

Putting her book down beside her, leaving it open at her place, Tippy struggled with a conversation she'd never before had. She'd have told him again he was American if that would end it, but no confrontation in which Bidziil's body shook ended that easily. "If you have to think of yourself as anything more than American..."

"I do!"

"I don't," said Tippy, "but if you want to think of something else, then your first mother and first father were Native Americans."

Bidziil stared at her, his eyes locked on hers but also looking not into her, but through her, as if she wasn't really there. Slowly, he slipped down to the floor. There, he sat with his knees up, legs together, and arms around his legs, staring somewhere in front of him.

From her chair, Tippy looked down on him: small again sitting bunched up on the floor, in a room that he made seem very big for him being very small. "Do you know about Native Americans?" Tippy asked him.

"My teacher talked about them," he answered, without looking up at her. "I didn't know she meant me."

Tippy watched him, not knowing what he felt or what to say. Should she tell him that being Native American didn't matter, or that it did, but mattered less than being an American? She thought of telling him she wished that she was Native American, but that would be telling him it mattered.

Bidziil looked up at her. "What are you?" he asked her.

"I'm an American, like you are."

"You're not like I am, are you?"

If his was the position of the student child seated on the floor and hers was that of the teacher parent seated in her chair, a book beside her, then she wasn't doing well. She had taught him to master challenges, from walking through to writing and reading, among everything else of which a child knows nothing and a parent knows far more than she realized, until she is called upon to teach it. He might have had more to teach her than she had to teach him.

"What then are you?" asked Bidziil, pressing the point.

Her eyes remained on his eyes, looking at them as they looked at her, except that his eyes looked expectantly at her and she could not look expectantly on him, so young. He, the child, was entitled to look to her for answers as she could not look to him.

Slowly, Tippy came to look not into him but through him, as if he wasn't really there, into a space apart from him. Whatever was right or wrong in Tippy's adult mind mattered less than Bidziil's childish expectations. In the face of his innate conviction, uncluttered by whatever life had cluttered in her, her conviction no longer seemed as valid as it had.

Tippy whispered, so that only Bidziil heard her and so that she could tell him afterwards he'd misheard her, if she had a chance to start that afternoon again. "If you have to think of me as anything more than American," she whispered, but that choice of words seemed strangely insensitive, foisting all responsibility on him, "if I have to think of myself as anything more than American, and I suppose I do, then I am white. I am European. I am English."

5 FINDING KIN

When white people stopped believing in race, they stopped believing in biological connections between people. They believed that families could be whatever they wanted them to be.

Thus in modern-day Seattle, Tippy Norton (with her husband Hywell Oakland) adopted Native American baby Bidziil without thought of race. In time, Bidziil reached the age to contrast himself with other people. He began learning about race.

Bidziil also learned to communicate, and communicated that contrast between him and people of other races with his adoptive mother. Strange as it may seem, Tippy needed an adoptive child to teach her that she was white: an English American, to turn the phrase describing Bidziil. It took her to being in her late twenties to learn, but she too began learning about race.

Growing up, Bidziil wanted to read at home books about Native Americans like the ones he read at school. Tippy bought them because she bought any books that Bidziil said he'd read. She read them too, if only to learn more about him.

Bidziil listened to Native American music, as Tippy also listened. (For all her prior knowledge and affection for Native Americans, even without appreciating she was thinking about race, she'd previously been unaware of Native American music.) With everything Bidziil learnt about himself, Tippy learnt about him too.

Together in their home, Tippy and Bidziil watched movies about Native Americans: modern movies more than older movies. After they'd watched one particular movie, Tippy said to Bidziil, "Yours are a fine and noble people."

He turned towards her. "Are yours a fine and noble people?" he asked her.

Tippy looked away. "I never considered it," she answered.

"Why did you consider it about my people, if you didn't consider it about yours?"

He could make her most uncomfortable. "It's not the sort of thing we think about," Tippy told him.

"Why don't you think about it?"

She looked back at him, whom she loved and to whom she gave so much, in his comfortable surrounds. "Why don't I think about it?"

Tippy began to read old American and English books (by which she meant anything written before her grandparents were born), watch old American and British films (by which she meant anything produced before her parents were born), and listen to old American and European music (by which she meant anything composed before she was born). She could not help but learn about herself.

No longer denying race, Tippy celebrated it, but only within her family home and only to herself. She celebrated diversity because that's what Americans did with diversity, telling Bidziil theirs was a rainbow family.

Hywell's first family was not like that. With her four adult stepchildren living elsewhere, more of them becoming married and bearing children over time, its legacy in Tippy's home was a single photograph of them with their father and late mother. The portrait of six stood in a silver frame on a sideboard in the formal dining room for Hywell and his visiting children with their families to see, but Tippy and Bidziil not to see all the time.

Tippy kept her learning to herself. Just as she never mentioned Bidziil being Native American, even to people seeing him or asking after his unusual name, she never mentioned her whiteness, her Englishness. She never spoke of race with Hywell, fifteen years her senior and still busy with his business, or with her stepchildren. They too had never spoken of being white, or English, in her presence. The only person who spoke of race, so far as Tippy ever heard, was Bidziil.

To everyone, except Bidziil, Tippy remained what she had always been: American. To Tippy, everyone remained American, except that Bidziil was also Native American and she was also English.

For the most part in all apparent respects, Bidziil behaved like a typical American boy. In spite of Tippy's additional tutoring, his grades at school were below average, but some children's grades had to be. He spent a short time in Boy Scouts and played basketball at school, although he was shorter than most other basketballers. Tippy drove him everywhere he needed to be, watched him practice and play, and drove him back home afterwards.

Hywell saw him practice and play less often, but still saw him when he could; he'd been the same with all his children, they told Tippy. He could have retired and Tippy never understood why he didn't, but his business still commanded much of his time. He, Tippy, and Bidziil shared their evenings and weekends together, as well as several vacations every year.

With Bidziil becoming older, those vacations became even more exotic. Hywell and Tippy showed him all the inhabited continents on earth, along with several islands in the Caribbean. None of the peoples they encountered diminished Bidziil's interest in his people. He never wavered from referring to Native Americans collectively as "us" or "we." Tippy slowly learned to refer to them in conversation with him as "you."

Tippy appreciated the pleasure of coming home to American soil, which Bidziil referred to as being "my" land. Thus Tippy spoke of it to him as "our" land and country: theirs and every other American's. She listened for Bidziil to say the same, without ever forcing the point upon him. He never did.

In a conversation between them about one pending vacation, Bidziil described England as "your homeland" and the English collectively as "you." Tippy sat silently, staring at him, as she often did.

With them all getting older, Tippy slowed. Passing thirty-nine years of age too soon, she became increasingly content to rest in their comfortable Seattle home, instead of busying herself in restaurants and cafés between tables of passing strangers. Being older still, Hywell slowed more than she slowed, with the first hint of a time coming in which the man who'd looked after her since their marriage might need looking after too.

Meanwhile, Bidziil quickened, needing Tippy less with every year. He enrolled in a driver education course and, at his third attempt, passed the test for his learner's permit.

What might be the last gesture Tippy could do for him, she sat with Bidziil learning to drive, day and night. On his fourth attempt, he obtained a driver's license.

Hywell and Tippy bought Bidziil a small car, because the parents they knew bought cars for their children. It was something more that Bidziil enjoyed in his childhood that Tippy's late parents had been unable to buy for hers.

Nothing better expressed Bidziil's maturity than Tippy obtaining for him a key to the front door of their home. He didn't really need a key, since Tippy was always home when he returned there and, if he came home at night, Hywell was also there. Even upon the rare occasions Hywell and Tippy were out somewhere, Bidziil knew that Tippy left the laundry door behind their house unlocked and knew the combination for the security system. The key was a token not just that Bidziil was mature enough to be an owner of their home, but that Tippy recognized he was.

Bidziil no longer needed Tippy to get anywhere or be anywhere, although she continued attending every parent event at Bidziil's school. If it seemed she saw too little of him, it was because American parents saw little of their children.

Soon enough, Bidziil entered his final year of high school. He was almost eighteen years of age.

Among the rooms in their home that decades earlier had been a bedroom, when Hywell and his first wife raised their four children, was Tippy's cozy tapestry room: a room as private to her as Hywell's study remained private to him. There alone, she sat threading a colorful tapestry the day that Bidziil bounded in, late home from school. "I've got a friend," he told her.

Tippy continued threading her tapestry. "You've got many friends," she pointed out.

"This is a real friend, someone like me."

Tippy looked up. "Your other friends are like you," she told him. Tippy stopped threading her tapestry.

Bidziil shook his head. "I saw her when she entered the class, obviously Native American."

There had been a time that Tippy would have asked what made someone obviously Native American. She no longer needed to do so.

"She saw me at my desk," beamed Bidziil, "and smiled as I must have smiled. I would have spoken to her then, but the teacher was there and the class began. She sat down and we looked at each other, as the teacher began talking about how fortunate the school was to have Native Americans among the school community. Any other day, I would have thought the teacher was talking only about me, the way teachers do, but the teacher asked if there were any Native Americans in the class and the two of us put up our hands.

The teacher asked everyone to clap and they did. Her name is Mansi."

Tippy smiled because smiling always seemed the best response, but she struggled to know how more to respond. "If you're happy," she told him, "then I'm happy."

"I'm happy," he roared, spinning around in his place, before running out of the room as he'd not run inside the house or anywhere else, except a basketball court, for years. Whether that was the happiest that Bidziil had ever been, it was certainly the most happiness he had ever conveyed to Tippy.

Bidziil and Mansi quickly became the best of friends; Mansi wasn't her legal name, but that was the name her grandmother called her and so was the name she called herself. She introduced Bidziil to her parents.

Standing in her bathroom, Tippy was affixing make-up to her face when Bidziil returned home. "Mansi only has one father," Bidziil told her. "She only has one mother."

Tippy didn't really like anyone else being in the bathroom when she was adjusting her make-up, becoming a little more involved each year. (Tippy only tinted her hair, keeping its color, when she was the only person at home, as she increasingly was.) "Poor Mansi," said Tippy.

Bidziil stood silently. Finally, he left the room.

When she had finished tending to her face, Tippy found Bidziil lying on his bed in his bedroom. "Why don't you invite Mansi to come here?" she asked him.

"It's different here."

"Your father and I would dearly like to meet her."

"Like you dearly wanted to meet me," asked Bidziil, "almost eighteen years ago?"

Tippy didn't understand his answer. She didn't understand his question.

Bidziil stood up from his bed and went to his desk, where he sat down and opened a book. Tippy had often pressed him to study, so shouldn't press him to maintain their conversation. She left his room, closing the door after her.

There nevertheless seemed to be no warning for the day that Tippy, drinking coffee in their breakfast area at home, was approached by Bidziil so serious in his manner. "I want to find my father," he told her, "my mother."

Putting her cup of coffee down, Tippy reached her arms towards him. "I am your mother…"

"You are not my mother," he rebuked her, pulling away.

This was not merely the distinction between Bidziil's first mother and his second, which he had occasionally brought up in context over the years. This was, for the first time, denying Tippy was his mother at all. "I love you, Bidziil," she told him.

"Loving me doesn't make you my mother," answered Bidziil. "It makes you someone who loves me."

He had made loving him inadequate, as it had never before been, not to Tippy. "I raised you Bidziil, as if you were my child," she told him, proving herself, she felt. "I never treated you as anything else. I have been everything a mother can be."

"Not everything," Bidziil corrected her. "You're not anything a mother is. You've not done anything a mother does to be a mother. You've been a nurse, a teacher, a provider, and I thank you, but none of those people are mothers."

They were strange words to hear from Bidziil, not just in sentiment but in vocabulary. "Who have you been listening to?" she asked him.

"Me."

Tippy knew he had listened to someone more than that. "Your other mother couldn't care for you," she told him, "couldn't nurture you."

Bidziil's eyes flared at her. "She's not my other mother," he corrected her. "She's my mother. You're…something else."

He left Tippy alone, watching the empty space through which he'd gone. She would still refer to him as her son, but she rarely met anyone new anymore so rarely had cause to refer to him as anything but Bidziil. Her coffee went cold.

Bidziil remained polite to Tippy and Hywell, but began calling her "Tippy" and calling him "Hywell" as if they were his friends, not his parents. Conversations between them didn't need Bidziil to speak of them being his mother and father, but Tippy overheard him speaking on his telephone refer to her as the woman looking after him.

Tippy had long lost the biographies she and Hywell had been given about Bidziil's parents before they adopted him; she had probably thrown them out soon after receiving them. Nevertheless, in what seemed the only gesture she could make to reach Bidziil, she obtained another copy from the adoption service.

She found Bidziil sitting at his computer in his bedroom, where she gave that copy of their biographies to him. Bidziil took the sheet of paper from her, stood up from his desk, and stepped away from her. Beside the window and all that open space outside, he held that introduction to his parents in both his hands.

Their biographies were rather short, without their names or other identification except their tribes, but Bidziil took much longer than he needed to read them. If reading that sheet of paper for so long was supposed to make it longer, it didn't. If reading it for so long taught him more about his parents, then he did not say so to Tippy.

Without speaking, Bidziil turned back from the widow. He walked around Tippy to the door of his bedroom and out.

From a distance, she followed him downstairs and to the rear of the house, where he stepped outside, closing the door behind him. Tippy didn't follow him outside.

From a window, she watched him. Bidziil sat down on the grass, his legs crossed in front of him, with that piece of paper still in his hand at his side. He faced away from Tippy and their home, so she could not see whether his eyes were open. She imagined them being closed, because she imagined him thinking without thought of her, Hywell, or the house from which he'd turned.

There he sat, while Tippy watched, unwilling and probably unable to disturb him. When the afternoon became dark, Tippy switched on the house lights, but not the garden lights; she didn't think he wanted to be reminded of the house, or her.

Nor did Tippy tell him when she was serving dinner. As she did when he wasn't home to eat meals with her and Hywell, when Hywell was home, Tippy served his meal on a plate she stood on the kitchen bench. When his meal had cooled to room temperature, and the room temperature was becoming cool with winter nearing, but he'd still not returned to eat it, Tippy wrapped his plate and meal in plastic to stow in the refrigerator. She would reheat it in the oven when he was ready to reheat it.

The meal remained in the refrigerator. Bidziil remained in the cold outside, seated on the grass, facing away from her and their home.

When Tippy and Hywell retired to bed, she left lights shining in the house to lead Bidziil in, as she normally did of a night when he was not yet home. He could reheat his dinner when he wanted it.

It might have been any night with Hywell sleeping beside her in their bed that Bidziil was out somewhere, without Tippy knowing when Bidziil would return, except this night he was close by and Tippy lay awake. Finally, she heard the opening and closing door of Bidziil returning to the house. His footsteps followed.

Tippy rose from her and Hywell's bed, stepped across their bedroom, and stood at their open bedroom door, from which the top of the stairs was in view. Lights downstairs extinguished, before she heard the creaks and steps of Bidziil slowly coming up.

At the top of the stairs, he saw Tippy watching him and stopped. "My parents' biographies are mine," he whispered through the dead of night, "except that my mother's tribe isn't mine, nor is my father's tribe mine, because they weren't of the one tribe. That's the reason I am here, instead of being with both of them. That's the reason I was available for you to snatch."

Tippy had no sensible response. She had no response at all.

Bidziil returned to his bedroom. He closed the door.

Through the ensuing days and weeks, Tippy waited for him to elaborate or otherwise continue that line of exposition, but he never did. Bidziil never said anything more about those biographies to Tippy or to Hywell, Hywell told her. She would not intrude upon Bidziil by asking, when all she knew to ask were his feelings and she could not ask him about them. What he must have decided was none of her concern, but still every bit her concern. All she knew to do was all she ever knew to do with him: love him, support him, and when she could spoil him.

For Bidziil's eighteenth birthday, Tippy bought a special large cake from the best bakery she knew, bringing it home in its shining white box more carefully than she might have previously brought anything home, since she and Hywell first brought baby Bidziil home. Scrolled in white icing across Bidziil's favorite chocolate icing was his name, along with Tippy and Hywell's love and best wishes for a happy birthday.

Delicately, Tippy set the resplendent cake in the center of the dining table in the formal dining room. Most delicately of all, she stood eighteen candles in a circle around the icing.

From a sideboard cupboard, Tippy brought out three small plates of their finest porcelain, which she normally only brought out for guests more formal than her family, and set them on the table by the cake. From the sideboard cutlery drawer keeping their finest sterling silver, she took three small forks she set beside the plates. Finally, she placed a small box of matches on the table beside the cake, waiting for the birthday boy, or birthday man, and Hywell, headed home early that day.

Bidziil arrived home before Hywell did, whereby Tippy led him to the dining room and table; her and Hywell's presents she'd given him that morning. However she expected him to respond to the resplendent cake she hadn't thought, but all he did was stand staring down at it. Feeling very short beside him, Tippy waited for him to speak.

"I have to leave," said Bidziil, still looking at the cake.

"I thought we'd have dinner at a nice restaurant," said Tippy, "your favorite. Would you like to invite Mansi?"

"I have to leave here, forever."

Tippy stared at him. He continued looking at the cake.

"I'm old enough to leave school, now," said Bidziil. "I know you think I'm going to college, but I'm not. If I can't find my mother or my father, I can find others among my people."

"We are your people."

Bidziil turned to face her. "You're English," he told her. "I'm Native American."

She might have found the moment easier to bear if he was angry with her, if his words were thrown out in rage amidst the arguments sometimes between them, but they weren't. They were simply a fact, in response to which Tippy offered a fact of her own. "I love you, Bidziil."

"You don't know me."

"I've known you since you were born."

"You've never known me. You don't know my people."

"I know you," pleaded Tippy. "I know what's inside you."

"My nation is inside me."

"Our nation," said Tippy.

"Your nation isn't my nation." If Tippy had forgotten, then Bidziil never had.

"We raised you," she told him.

"Do you want a thank-you card?" asked Bidziil. "Do you want me to give up my life to thank you? I don't owe you anything."

"I owe you, Bidziil," Tippy smiled at him.

The smiles that still persuaded Hywell no longer affected

Bidziil. "I'm not looking for anything from you," said Bidziil, "but the chance to leave." He left the dining room.

Tippy followed him to the foot of the stairs. From there, she watched him climb the stairs to his bedroom.

He soon reappeared dragging a suitcase: a family suitcase they'd used for vacations, with wheels in a corner to drag along. He must have packed it that morning, or earlier; she'd not been in his room that day.

Tippy watched him coming down the stairs towards her, but not really towards her, carrying his suitcase. "Your father will be home soon," she told him.

"You can tell Hywell I've gone."

Bidziil reached her at the foot of the stairs. Tippy instinctively stepped back to let him pass her, before realizing she shouldn't have.

Dragging the suitcase on its wheels, which had never seemed to squeak until then, Bidziil proceeded along the hallway. At the mirror, near the front door, Bidziil paused to see his reflection. From his shirt pocket, he pulled out his ring of keys. "Can I keep the car?" he asked.

"It was always yours."

From his ring of keys, Bidziil removed a key. Placing it on the small thin table against the wall, Tippy saw which key it was.

"You can keep the house key, too," she told him. "You will always have a home here."

Bidziil faced her, along the hallway of her home. "I never had a home here," he told her.

"You need a place to live."

"I'm trying to find a place to live. Mansi's family has a spare room."

"You have no money."

He turned from her. He started walking the short distance left before the door.

"I'll give you money," Tippy told him.

He stopped walking. Tippy went to that small table and picked up her handbag. From her purse, she took every bill and coin to offer him. Bidziil stuffed them in his pocket.

"Any time you need more," said Tippy, "come here, call me, I can meet you."

Again, Bidziil turned from her. He proceeded to the door.

"Bidziil," said Tippy.

He stopped again, still facing the door in front of him. He stood his suitcase upright, releasing his hand from the handle.

"If Mansi were not a girl but a boy," said Tippy, "a Native American boy, would you be going there now?"

"This isn't about that. It's about family."

"Should we have adopted more children for you?" asked Tippy. "Should we have adopted more Native American children?"

"Do you think I am like you?" asked Bidziil, still facing the door. "Do you think I think only of me and my feelings, instead of those of my people: that I would want them to grow up as I have grown up, in another people's home, so I wouldn't be as much alone, but have company in my loneliness?"

Tippy continued staring at the back of him. "Were you alone, Bidziil?" she asked him.

He sighed. "I know you tried," he answered, "I know you both tried, and no one else in your position could have done more than you two did, but none of us could change that position."

Whether Tippy had failed, she didn't know. She hadn't failed at what she could have never done anyway. "Would it be any different if a Native American couple had adopted you," she asked him, "if Hywell and I were Native American?"

Bidziil stood still, facing away from her. "If you were Native American," he answered, "we'd have common ancestors. I'd need you to be of my tribe, my nation, for us to be really connected, closely connected, but if you were Native American, then we would be distantly connected. I could stay here, or you could come with me now, but you're not."

If staring at the back of him would keep him there, then Tippy would stare at him forever. "If there is any way I can be Native American," she told him, "I will be."

He laughed. "You are what your ancestors made you," he told her, as he reached his arms and hands to the door, unlocking it. "I am what my ancestors made me, and my ancestors aren't yours, which nobody can change."

"I love you, Bidziil," Tippy called to the back of him.

Bidziil opened the door. Dragging his suitcase on its small wheels, he stepped outside.

"Can I come with you, Bidziil?" Tippy begged of him.

He closed the door behind him. It locked automatically.

Tippy stood alone. The house was empty. She was too. "Bidziil!" she cried out. If he heard her, he didn't respond.

She was often alone in her home, but never before like this. No gardener, or cleaning maid, or laundrywoman, was due to come that day; she'd have been glad to see any one of them. The shingles on the roof were probably due for checking; she should bring that man back again.

Listlessly, without thought of all the leisure that ordinarily filled her days, Tippy ambled back to the dining room. Lying uneaten on the dining table was Bidziil's birthday cake, its eighteen untouched candles in a circle. She took the small box of matches and in turn, lit each of those candles.

In a fine dining chair among six the same, Tippy sat beside her flaming cake. Her company was her and Hywell's wishes scrolled in white icing over brown, close enough to talk with if those wishes made conversation back. Her voice softened, resigned to her being the only person hearing her. "Happy Birthday," she whispered, "Bidziil."

He was eighteen years of age, somewhere else; Tippy had never learnt where Mansi lived. Bidziil had never brought her to that house. Tippy hadn't met her.

Tippy would soon be forty-three years of age. Hywell would soon be fifty-eight.

She let the candles burn. If those eighteen burning candles spilt wax on Bidziil's cake, then nobody would care. Children might have cared, but adults wouldn't. With the sun soon due to set, those candles would be the best light with her.

Beyond the burning candles on the cake, Tippy saw again the single photograph of Hywell with his late wife and their four young children, now long grown up with children of their own. When any of them were next due to come for dinner or for any other reason Tippy could not recall, but it should be very soon.

Bidziil too had now grown up, but he would not be visiting. All any mother should want of her child is to grow up enough not to need her anymore, in which event the well-raised child should return for the same reason her husband's children and grandchildren visited: because they wanted to visit, or perhaps because their father and grandfather needed them instead of them needing him.

So Tippy remained there, in the afternoon becoming dark,

seated at that table for six: the family size of Hywell with his late wife and their children, but way too big for just him, Tippy, and Bidziil and way, way too big for just Hywell and Tippy.

Tippy might never before have seen birthday cake candles burning out. Birthday people normally blew them out too soon, amidst cries for happiness that might or might not be true.

A lowering flame finally lowered no more. It flickered and it died. The first flame to die made little difference, but the more flames that died the more they mattered, until finally those last few flames cast very little light. The last of them surrendered, and the room and house were dark.

Enough suburban lights appeared outside the windows to assure Tippy the windows were still there, that she was still at home. That photograph of her husband and stepchildren, with the mother of the house preceding her, remained vivid in the nighttime of her mind. If Bidziil was right about familial matters then, with their common ancestors, Tippy was distantly connected to all those people in the photograph.

The door from the garage opened. An electric light shone from there, casting a little sense of light along the hallway outside the open dining room door.

That was Hywell coming home early, but it wasn't really very early. He could have retired from work, whereby he would have been home when Bidziil came and went. He could have retired years ago.

The steps of Hywell walking along the hallway preceded another light shining there. The dining room became visible, if not the images of Hywell's late first wife and children.

In his business suit, Hywell walked past the open dining room door, doubtlessly not expecting Tippy to be there. Another light around a corner shone: the lounge room light.

The footsteps paused before soon starting again, as they might if Hywell was searching for her. Hywell appeared at the dining room door, switched on the light, and stood facing Tippy at the dining table, with the untouched birthday cake.

The candles on the cake had long burnt out, but those candles weren't important. They weren't Tippy or Hywell's candles, or the candles of any child of theirs.

"Where's Bidziil?" asked Hywell.

"Bidziil's gone, to be with his people. We might not see him again."

Hywell gazed down at her. "How are you feeling?" he asked her.

She smiled. "I'm with my people," she said, standing from her chair. She stepped towards him, reached up to him, and placed her hands against his cheeks as she'd not placed them for years. She kissed him.

His arms tentatively around her, he slowly came to hold her, kissing her. They kissed more fervently than they might have kissed for years, as they might have kissed when they'd met if they'd met when they were young, but they'd not met when they were young. The kiss was long, belying their ages, longer than every other kiss they might have shared all rolled into one, in that moment of their youths that never was.

When Tippy tired, she pulled back her hands from his face and stepped away. Hywell let her go, watching her.

They both dropped their arms and hands so that Tippy took Hywell's hand. She stepped to the side and turned, so they stood beside each other, holding each other's hands. There, they faced together that mammoth dining table. Remaining uneaten was that hefty birthday cake, a little less resplendent for the burnt candles around the icing but still with sweet tastes around it and inside it. At the ready were those fine porcelain plates and sterling silver forks.

Tippy's smaller woman's hand gently squeezed Hywell's larger man's hand. "Shall we go upstairs?"

6 MISCEGENATION

Piers LeBlanc felt certain he'd have loved jazz music wherever he'd grown up. Growing up within earshot of New Orleans made his love inescapable. It was love that led him to donate large sums of money to the Preservation Hall on St Peter Street. Providing for not just the best musicians but those trying to be the best kept the music sounding, although they'd have played for free.

His donations, more than being a middle-aged doctor in another part of New Orleans, brought Piers and his wife Lily-Anne invitations like the one to the Saturday dinner at the Royal Sonesta Hotel, Bourbon Street. Along with his black dinner suit, Piers wore his red silk waistcoat from the left pocket of which hung his silver fob watch, for no other reason than his late father wore them. He always moved a little slower when he did.

With a bevy of dignitaries, speaker after speaker denounced racism against the city's majority black population. Most speakers, including Piers, were white; the audience particularly liked hearing white people denounce racism and white people particularly liked doing so.

With the diners finishing their main dishes and Piers having finished his, he stepped up to the podium. Standing at the microphone, he stared out around the ballroom of men and women dressed in their evening best, while waiters and waitresses moved about the tables, removing plates and filling glasses. "Without Africans," Piers addressed them, "we'd have no jazz. Without jazz, we'd have no New Orleans."

Diners clapped. Piers had become a little carried away with the words he'd rehearsed for days on end, but nobody bothered with the details of what he said. Sentiment mattered, and his was the sentiment they'd come to hear.

The clapping slowly abated. "In my medical profession," resumed Piers, "we have the Hippocratic Oath. That oath compels doctors to treat patients without recourse to the color of their skin." Piers hadn't actually read the oath since making it (and he must have made it for other doctors to mention it and others to mention it on their behalf), but he felt certain it said as much. "In New Orleans, we make the Hippocratic Oath not simply as doctors to our patients, but as human beings to each other."

Again, the diners clapped. At the back of the ballroom, beyond those tables of people clapping, appeared a handsome young man nicely dressed in a lounge suit, if not as nicely dressed as other, primarily older, men in the room. Piers hadn't expected to see his son Ryder there that night.

Standing beside Ryder, apparently their arms around each other, was a young woman Piers didn't recognize. She wore a long elegant dress not as extravagant as those that other, primarily older, women wore in the room, but comparable in elegance to Ryder's suit. As perhaps Piers should have noticed given the theme of the evening, or as perhaps he should not have noticed given the theme, she was black: not completely black, as recent immigrants often were, but black enough to be black.

Ryder was nineteen years old, still living with his parents. He'd had a few girlfriends over time, as distinct from his female friends, but he'd kept them away from his parents; Piers and Lily-Anne only learnt of them from Ryder's younger sisters. They'd not mentioned any of those girlfriends being black, and perhaps they'd not have thought to mention it if any of them was. This was the first time Piers had seen Ryder with a woman apparently his girlfriend.

The applause had largely abated before Piers noticed it abating. The words he had rehearsed had slipped far from his mind, as he looked back around the ballroom. He smiled, trying to think of what more he'd planned to say, but couldn't. "Thank you," he said, stepping from the podium.

His speech had been the shortest made that evening, but there'd been a lot of speeches and might be more, so Piers felt certain nobody would mind. He returned to a large round table much like any other and his chair beside his wife.

Lily-Anne leant close to him. "That was very good, darling," she whispered, while Piers sat watched their son looking towards them and the stranger standing close beside him, perhaps closer than they'd previously stood. There was no space for Ryder's arm or hers between them. Their arms must have been around each other.

"Do you know that woman with Ryder?" Piers asked Lily-Anne.

She began to turn around. "Don't look now," Piers stopped her. "Look when he and she won't notice."

Piers' face turned a small way from being pointed towards his son and the woman while remaining generally towards the rear of the room. His concentration remained upon those whom his eyes would not identify.

Piers and Lily-Anne sat silently. Conversation with other diners at the table would have been awkward when simply sitting there was awkward.

Lilly-Anne prepared to stand. Piers stood with her, pulling her chair back from the table to help her stand, as he always did. "I'll see," she said, as she walked away.

Piers watched her head generally towards the rear of the room, before she veered around one table and between more tables towards, Piers slowly realized, an exit and the women's restroom. Alone, he stared as if he wasn't staring at anything, but he was staring at his son and the woman with him.

The speeches concluded. Diners finished their meals. A waitress offered Piers coffee but he declined, although he accepted one for Lily-Anne: black.

When Lily-Anne returned to the ballroom and ultimately their table, Piers stood momentarily for her, as he always did, pushing her chair under her as she sat. "Thank you, darling," she said, sipping her coffee.

"Did you see her?" asked Piers.

"I didn't recognize her. Ryder has black female friends, but I didn't recognize this one."

"He knew we'd be here," said Piers. "I knew he was going out somewhere tonight, but I've stopped asking where he goes. They can't be attending the dinner or they'd be at a table. They must have slipped in late knowing nobody would mind."

"If it's bothering you, approach them."

"Should we?" asked Piers. The only matters about which Piers asked his wife for advice were those concerning their children.

"We could."

"Should we?"

"Both of us approaching them might intimidate her," said Lily-Anne.

"It might intimidate him," said Piers, again looking towards his son. "It might intimidate me."

Asking Lily-Anne to approach them seemed ungentlemanly, and Piers was always gentlemanly. He pushed back his chair and stood up, as Lily-Anne again sipped her coffee.

"I'll tell you what they say," said Piers.

With no reason to conceal his observation, Piers faced Ryder and the woman with him at the rear of the room, as he made his way towards them. Moments here and there, he looked down at the chairs and tables he stepped behind and around, but for the most part his eyes remained upon them.

Ryder, his arm still apparently around the woman and her arm still apparently around him, watched Piers coming. His lips seemed to say something. She too was watching Piers.

Between the last of the tables and the wall against which they stood, was plenty of carpeted space. "Son," said Piers as he reached them, by way of introducing himself to the woman. He looked at her and smiled. "Miss," he addressed her, in the absence of a name.

Their arms around each other, Ryder responded. "Dad," he said, "this is Jasmine."

"Hello, Jasmine," smiled Piers. He didn't normally shake the hands of young women, or otherwise greet them with anything more than words, but he had a point to make. He offered Jasmine his hand to shake.

That necessitated her pulling her arm from behind Ryder and him pulling his arm from behind her, although that wasn't Piers' idea. She offered Piers her hand to shake.

Ever so gently, Piers shook her hand, bowing slightly as he did. She smiled, as they each pulled their hands away.

"Jasmine wanted to hear your speech tonight," Ryder explained.

"Did you mean what you said?" asked Jasmine, with an accent as Louisianan as any other. "Did any of the speakers, the white ones, mean what they said?"

"I meant it," answered Piers. "All the speakers were sincere, without question, including the white ones."

"Why don't you prove it?" asked Jasmine. "Why don't you stand back up there at the microphone and tell everyone your big white boy's going out with a little black girl?"

If her manner was much too confrontational, Piers did not reciprocate. Instead, he shook his head. "You're not little," he smiled. She was almost Ryder's height, and he wasn't little. "Ryder's not big," he continued, although at nineteen years of age he was close to it. "The speeches are over."

She continued staring at him, edging back close to Ryder and putting her arm back around him, as he put his arm back around her. "You'll forgive me," she told Piers, "if I'm used to white folks saying one thing about black people but acting another."

"Ryder's white," Piers reminded her.

"He's proven his goodness, to me."

"How can I prove my goodness?" asked Piers. "Returning to the podium now empty and seizing a microphone that has probably been switched off would embarrass you, and I think embarrass Ryder and me too."

Again Jasmine stared at Piers, before answering. "I shouldn't have to think up a test," she told him. "You should."

Piers opened his arms. His eyes left her to look around them for a clue.

All the while, Ryder stood silently, watching him, with his arm around Jasmine and hers around him. Jasmine held him in a way that plainly his parents no longer could.

Finally, Piers shook his head. "Give me time," he told her.

"Until then," answered Jasmine, "you haven't proved a thing."

Feeling something of a failure, Piers deferred to the best counsel he knew for personal problems. "May I introduce you to Ryder's mother?" he asked Jasmine.

Piers looked back across the room to Lily-Anne, watching them. Her and Piers' table was becoming empty, in a room of tables becoming empty.

"Can she prove her goodness?" asked Jasmine.

Piers turned back to Jasmine. "She proves her goodness more often than any other person I know," he told her.

"Is that goodness just for white people, or black people too?"

"She's good to everyone," Piers assured her, Jasmine's arm still around Ryder and his arm still around her. "We're not a family that thinks about race."

"White people don't have to think about race," responded Jasmine, "but do anyway. Black people have to think about race, all the time."

"Not with me, you don't," smiled Piers. "Not with Ryder's mother, you don't."

"Prove it."

"Come with me," said Piers, stepping back and holding his arm towards the distant table at which Lily-Anne sat. "Meet Ryder's mother."

Jasmine looked towards Lily-Anne for a moment, before dropping her arm from behind Ryder. She left Ryder's arm dangling behind her.

She led the way between tables and around chairs, most of them empty. Ryder and then Piers followed her.

The only person left sitting at her table, Lily-Anne watched them approach. As they neared, Lily-Anne stood up, as she only did for women approaching her at a table.

At the table, Jasmine sat in a chair near, but not nearest, to Lily-Anne, who then sat back down. Jasmine reached forward across the table and took a small chocolate from a plate, before sitting back in her chair. Ryder sat beside Jasmine, on the far side from his mother.

"This is Jasmine," Piers introduced her to his wife, as he returned to the chair in which he'd sat earlier. "This is Mrs. LeBlanc," he said to Jasmine, as he always introduced young people to his wife.

"Please," Lily-Anne smiled at Jasmine, "call me Lily-Anne."

Ryder reached his hand below the table, towards Jasmine sitting beside him. It appeared, from where Piers sat, that he placed his hand on her leg.

"That is a lovely dress you're wearing," Lily-Anne told Jasmine. "You do look very graceful."

"We have been to dinner," explained Jasmine, reaching forward to take another chocolate, "at Brennan's." She popped the chocolate in her mouth.

"Very nice," said Lily-Anne.

A waiter carrying a small coffee pot appeared beside her. He held the pot near Lily-Anne's cup.

"Thank you," said Lily-Anne.

After the waiter poured her cup, he offered it to Jasmine, who shook her head. He offered it to Ryder, who shook his head. He offered it to Piers.

"No, thank you," replied Piers. The waiter left them.

Again, Lily-Anne made the politest of conversation with Jasmine. "It's such a pleasure for us to meet you," smiled Lily-Anne. "I'm afraid Ryder doesn't tell us very much about his personal life."

"Ryder is my boyfriend," Jasmine told her, "if that's what you mean."

"How lovely," smiled Lily-Anne. "May I ask, not meaning to intrude, how you two met? I used to love it when people asked me where Ryder's father and I met."

"What makes you want to know?" Jasmine asked her. "It wasn't anywhere you have to worry about."

"I'm not worried…"

Jasmine had already turned to Piers. "I heard what you said about jazz in your speech," she told him. "Ryder gets jazz. He gets Africans in America. He gets me."

Piers smiled at her, while he thought of something to say. He thought of asking whether she understood Ryder, got him as she would say, but didn't know how to ask courteously. Piers should simply presume she did. "That's nice," he said.

Jasmine reached forward to take the last chocolate from the plate. "I've told Ryder I'm going to marry him," she said, popping that chocolate in her mouth.

Piers looked at Ryder. His son didn't flinch. Piers didn't need to face Lily-Anne to know she looked at Ryder too.

Unusually that evening, Ryder spoke. "I haven't asked Jasmine to marry me," he told his parents. Piers wasn't certain he believed him.

Jasmine spoke up; she was rarely out of the conversation very long. "I've told Ryder I don't want him to ask me to marry him," she told Piers, "until he's asked my father first, and I haven't told Ryder to do that, yet."

Piers looked at Lily-Anne. She turned to him, before turning back to Jasmine and smiling. "Would you and your parents like to come to our home for Sunday lunch?" she asked Jasmine. Lily-Anne convened all the entertaining at their family home. "Tomorrow might be too soon, but we'd be delighted if you could come next Sunday."

"We all go to church on Sunday," answered Jasmine, before looking back at Ryder, his hand still on her lap it seemed. "Ryder is coming with me tomorrow."

"I hadn't known," said Lily-Anne, a little more forthrightly than Piers normally saw from her, towards people outside her family. "We have a family church. Would you like to join us there Jasmine, one Sunday morning?"

Jasmine looked back at Lily-Anne; the table conversation had become one between them. "Ryder told me about his church," said Jasmine, "the people, singing, and preaching. It's a white people's church."

"We have black people in the congregation," said Lily-Anne.

"Black people out of touch with being black, with being African: preoccupied with rich white surroundings instead of their souls."

"You might reacquaint them with their souls," suggested Lily-Anne.

"If I did reacquaint them with their souls, they'd leave your church, or change it so much you would leave."

"We wouldn't leave," smiled Lily-Anne. "We love Africans and all things African."

"Would you love African grandchildren?"

Piers glanced at Ryder. Again, his son didn't flinch.

He looked back at Lily-Anne, who took another of her moments to sit quietly, preparing her words rather than saying something that would embarrass her or, worse than that, embarrass Jasmine. She then smiled, in the signal, if only to Piers, that she reached a solution. "You two are close."

Jasmine edged closer to Ryder. She rested her hand on his lap much as his hand apparently remained on hers.

"May we all come to your church Jasmine, one Sunday?" asked Lily-Anne.

"Don't expect us to change anything for you."

"We wouldn't," smiled Lily-Anne. "We would dearly love to host you and your family to lunch, or dinner, or something in our home, whenever suits you."

"Ryder showed me your home," said Jasmine, "during that weekend you were away."

Lily-Anne looked at Piers. He hadn't known.

"I didn't like it," continued Jasmine. "I felt alien there, with all your stuffy white people's books, paintings, and furniture."

Piers had never considered the books, paintings, and furniture in his home stuffy. He had never considered them being of white people.

"All I saw was stuffy white people's music," continued Jasmine. "Where was the jazz?"

Piers responded. "We listen to jazz live," he answered,

"including musicians who play in our home and gardens. We don't need recordings."

"I'm only interested in African music," said Jasmine. "So is Ryder."

Piers looked at Ryder. "I hadn't known," said Piers.

Jasmine responded. "You don't know your son," she told him. "We're only interested in African culture."

Piers continued looking at Ryder, who was curiously content to sit silently, looking at whoever was speaking. His hand remained on Jasmine's lap and her hand remained on his, like they were never going to leave.

"My parents have never been on a paddlewheeler," said Jasmine. "I have, with Ryder, but they haven't."

"The paddlewheelers aren't very African," Piers pointed out, in a moment of resistance.

"Neither is this hotel," answered Jasmine, looking up and around. Her eyes dwelt upon the crystal chandeliers hanging from the ceiling. Thus Piers' eyes dwelt upon them. "I could never stay here, but I'm willing to visit this room, with Ryder."

"Black people do stay here," Piers assured her.

"I don't listen to your music," Jasmine told him. "I don't stay in your hotels."

Piers looked back at Lily-Anne. "I never thought of music being ours," he said, as much to Jasmine as to anyone. He looked again around the ballroom. "I never thought of this hotel being ours."

"They're not mine," said Jasmine. "They're not my parents'. They won't be my children's."

"Won't they be your children's?" asked Piers, looking back at her. "If they're my wife's and mine, then they're Ryder's too. So won't they be his children's too?"

"No," snapped Jasmine, pulling her hand back from Ryder and sitting forward in her chair. His hand remained on her lap. "Our children will be African; Ryder agreed. African blood makes us African. White blood slips away."

A longer silence than usual followed, before Lily-Anne, always so gracious, spoke. "Jasmine," she said, "may we three host your parents and you to dinner on a paddlewheeler, this coming Saturday night? If you have brothers and sisters who would like to join us, I'm sure Ryder's sisters would like to meet you."

Jasmine sat back in her chair, returning her hand to Ryder's lap.

The ballroom was almost empty, with waiters and waitresses having cleared away other tables and the abandoned dinnerware from Piers and Lily-Anne's table, by then also Ryder and Jasmine's table. "I'll ask them," said Jasmine, standing up. "We should go."

They left Piers and Lily-Anne, the last dinner attendees still in the ballroom. Piers stood up, pulled Lily-Anne's chair from her, and waited while she stood.

"What do you think of that?" asked Lily-Anne, as they walked together towards the doors and exit.

"Not what I would have expected," replied Piers.

"We have to support him."

At their home again, in the old Garden District of New Orleans with its mansions and gardens, Piers poured himself a glass of bourbon whiskey from the cocktail cabinet in the lounge room. "I'll wait up for Ryder," he said.

"He is normally out late," said Lily-Anne, "later than this."

"I'll wait," said Piers, still dressed as he had been for the Royal Sonesta, settling into one of his comfortable old armchairs that Jasmine called stuffy. While sipping his neat whiskey, he admired his paintings from the past around the walls. His old books were in the library, out of Piers' sight just then, but Piers appreciated them without seeing them.

Marking time from a mantelpiece was a French antique clock. Jasmine must have hated that.

Whether it was for all being so pleasant, or for the time getting so late and being so tired, Piers fell asleep in his armchair, until a heavy door opening woke him. The time was almost three o'clock.

Piers stood up. "Ryder?" he said.

Moments later, Ryder appeared at the open lounge room door. His suit was a little crumpled, but so was Piers' suit.

"Jasmine made quite an impression," said Piers. "She thinks you're going to marry her."

"Women say these things."

"I hope you like our stuffy home."

"I never much thought about it."

Piers sat back down in his chair, still tired. "Neither had I," he admitted. "The man who built this house wasn't a relative of mine or your mother's, so far as we know, and we paid good money to buy it, but I'm thinking we inherited it anyway."

Ryder turned away. "I'm going to bed."

"Son," said Piers, drawing him back, "marriage is for the man and the woman. Children are for both their families."

Ryder departed. Creaking stairs and then the upstairs floorboards marked his passage to bed. They soon marked Piers' passage to bed.

By the time Piers and Lily-Anne woke in the morning, Ryder had already left the house. Piers and Lily-Anne attended their church with their daughters but without Ryder, which wasn't unusual.

The following days didn't teach Piers and Lily-Anne much more about Jasmine Moreau than the little they had previously learnt. She was the same age as Ryder and worked as a waitress in a restaurant at the university at which he studied. Two months earlier, they'd begun conversing when he sat alone with a meal and an assignment to finish. He'd not been to her home.

The next Saturday night, dressed as well as they ever dressed for a private dinner but no better (so Piers without his dinner suit, waistcoat, or fob watch), Piers and Lily-Anne waited with their two school-age daughters on a wharf by the Mississippi River. They stood by the steel gangplank leading to the *Creole Queen* paddlewheeler, which Piers and Lily-Anne never tired of dining upon, or just travelling upon. Jasmine's parents' and siblings' first trip on a paddlewheeler should be on one as long, tall, and old as the *Creole Queen*.

They didn't wait long before Ryder in his suit, Jasmine in another nice dress, and what was obviously her family arrived. Her father, of about Piers' height and build, wore a dark brown suit, almost fitting him. Her mother, of about Lily-Anne's height but with her hair brushed rather than set, wore a more modest long dress. Her brothers and sisters, five in all, wore neat but casual clothes: not quite as neat as and decidedly more casual than the long dresses Ryder's sisters wore.

"You're Piers," said Jasmine's father, reaching them. "Call me Zebedee." He offered him his hand to shake.

Piers accepted. "Thank you for joining us, Zebedee," he told him. "This is my wife, Lily-Anne."

Zebedee introduced his wife. "This is Esmerelda."

More introductions followed, including those for the children who stood apart from each other, staring. Zebedee then turned to a white lifebuoy marked with the name *Creole Queen*, hanging from a small post on a patch of carpet on the wharf. Enough tourists and people commemorating special events boarded each cruise for there to be a commercial photographer at the ready.

"Come here," Zebedee told his wife and children.

They followed him, as he mustered the eight of them together behind the lifebuoy for a photograph. There, conspicuously without Ryder, thought Piers, they grinned as brightly as any arriving passengers had.

The photograph taken, Zebedee's family dispersed, while he gave the photographer a name. "We're with Piers LeBlanc," he told her.

Piers led his party of thirteen in single file along the gangplank to the paddlewheeler, with its steam engines bubbling, paddlewheel turning, and water splashing back into the river. As was normally the case, a small group of musicians played jazz from a podium by the stairs; they were all tunes Piers recognized and never tired of hearing. The paddlewheeler soon moved away from the wharf.

Zebedee leant against the upstairs railing and gazed at the boats and shores they passed with awe and wonder Piers had long lost. Trying to make conversation, Piers talked of what they observed, until he realized he was imposing.

Near them, Lily-Anne talked with Esmerelda, looking around the vessel as people normally did their first time aboard; Piers remembered the times he did the same. Ryder stood with Jasmine, who still found enough of interest to look around. The children were elsewhere; the boat was big enough for Piers to lose sight of them.

Dinner brought them together, with the children at one large table and the adults at another. "Jasmine mentioned you attended church," said Piers, as much to Zebedee as Esmerelda.

Zebedee and Esmerelda continued looking past Piers and Lily-Anne at whatever the paddlewheeler passed. "We're Baptists," said Zebedee.

Lily-Anne joined the conversation. "We have visited some lovely Baptist churches," she said.

Zebedee continued gazing at the view. "Don't expect black Baptist churches to be like white Baptist churches," he replied. "We don't like people doing things we hear white Baptists don't mind them doing."

"I also don't like people doing those things," agreed Lily-Anne.

"We all worship the same God."

Zebedee looked away from the view towards Lily-Anne. "God made black folk," he said, "white folk, and all the other folk. Now, I've got nothing against white folk and nothing against them marrying into my family – I can't say that about other folk – but it won't do saying God meant us all to live the same way. I want to keep us our religion."

Piers responded. "We want you to keep your religion too," he told him.

"I've told Jasmine," said Zebedee, "your boy has to come to our church if he wants to sit in church with her, and she's not going out with any boy she can't sit in church with. Your boy will have to stop calling himself Catholic, but even calling himself Baptist won't do if it's not our kinda Baptist. I want our grandchildren raised in their heritage."

They all ordered their drinks. They ordered their food. Zebedee's words and sentiment played on Piers' mind.

After the waiter left, Piers resumed his conversation with Zebedee. "The Catholic church is almost two thousand years old," said Piers.

"Your name, LeBlanc, means white," said Zebedee. "I looked it up."

Piers already knew the French origin of his name and, he suspected, the name Moreau. "I think," said Piers, "we've always thought of ourselves as Louisianans."

"We're Louisianan too," said Zebedee, "and African. We like being African, have faith in being African. I want our grandchildren to look at a map of the world and see a place that's forever theirs: Africa. I don't want them seeing a map without seeing somewhere they know is theirs."

"Would you prefer that Jasmine marry an African?" asked Piers.

"Ryder has told my daughter that his ancestors aren't important to him, which is good, so France isn't going to affect my grandchildren. Europe ends with you. It ends with Ryder the day he marries Jasmine. Oh, I don't mind if he keeps those thoughts inside his head, but he told Jasmine he won't do that. I don't want them confusing my grandchildren."

Silence ensued. If Lily-Anne was trying to think of something she could say, she fared no better than Piers.

"I'm glad we can talk like this," said Zebedee. "It's good."

Piers continued staring at him, while words formed in his head. "We haven't thought enough about our heritage," he admitted, "so thank you for bringing it to my attention." He looked at Jasmine. "Thank you too, Jasmine."

"Glad to help," said Zebedee.

"We've also not thought enough about our grandchildren," Piers continued. "They seemed so far off, until last Saturday."

Zebedee laughed. "Jasmine will do that," he said.

"I think you're right in everything you've said," admitted Piers. "I don't want my grandchildren confused. I want them to look at a map and know they have an ancestral home. I want them to have identity, heritage, and culture without ambiguity."

Piers had said enough. Their meals had not yet come.

"Please, Zebedee," said Piers, "tell us more about being African."

Zebedee talked of history and music, in Africa and America. He talked of art more in Africa. He talked of Africans encouraging and discouraging him, of moments of hope and of despair.

All the while, Piers listened. He learnt about black Africans and slowly about Frenchmen. Listening to Zebedee describe his inherited riches, Piers came better to understand his inherited riches. None of those riches, for either man, related to money.

They ate. Zebedee and less often Esmerelda and Jasmine talked. Piers, Lily-Anne, and Ryder listened. Musicians played jazz music near them.

At the table beside theirs, the children talked. They seemed to get on well.

Piers paid for the evening cruise and meal; he and Lily-Anne had invited everyone. He paid for Zebedee's souvenir glossy photograph from the start of the evening, in a cushioned display folder, which Zebedee proudly showed to his family and then Piers' family.

At the end of the cruise, when the *Creole Queen* was nearing the wharf and passengers preparing to alight, Piers turned to Zebedee. "If Ryder wanted to maintain our family like the one he was born to," said Piers, "the way Jasmine wants to maintain your family like the one she was born to, then they can't marry each other, can they?"

Zebedee looked at Piers, before again looking around the paddlewheeler from which they would soon alight. He looked around as a man would look thinking he might never be in a place again. The side of the paddlewheeler nudged the wharf.

Their party of thirteen alighted as they had arrived: in single file back along the gangplank. On the reasonably well-lit wharf, while other past passengers dispersed into the night, Piers looked at Zebedee. "Thank you," smiled Piers.

Zebedee nodded. "I hope Jasmine and Ryder remain friends," he said.

"I think they will."

"Good night, Esmerelda," said Lily-Anne.

"Goodbye, Lily-Anne."

There were various more words of parting, including those between Ryder and Jasmine. "I'll call you tomorrow," he said to her. She reached close to him and they kissed, briefly.

Zebedee, carrying his souvenir photograph, and his family departed. On such a warm night, the wharf, like the river, remained busy.

Watching them go, only Lily-Anne and their children remained with Piers on the wharf. "I was wrong about the Hippocratic Oath," remarked Piers, when Jasmine and her family had walked far enough away.

"All of which means," said Ryder, "Jasmine should marry a black man, shouldn't she, and I must marry a white woman: French, or English with a touch of French?"

Piers turned to his son. "Were you ever planning to marry Jasmine?" asked Piers.

Ryder smiled. "I'm nineteen years old," he answered, putting his hand on his father's shoulder, "headed I hope to medical school. I'm not marrying anyone, yet."

7 LITERATURE

Whatever Americans meant when they spoke of judging people by what was inside them, it didn't mean their culture. Culture isn't race but it reflects race, so that people determined to ignore one ignore the other. People valuing their race value their culture too. People favoring other races favor other cultures too.

Like other white Americans, Franklin Knowles didn't think in terms of valuing his race, but he valued American arts and other culture more than most Americans did, even if he didn't think in terms of them being his culture. In the family home he and his wife made for them and their children in rural New Jersey was an extensive library of books. With so much else to do, Franklin was too slowly reading his way through it.

A generation earlier, when Franklin was at school, the best of his teachers were those who did more than impart knowledge. They inspired their students with loves for their disciplines for being important, insightful, and often beautiful. In English classes, that meant the best of American and other literature.

Two decades into the twenty-first century, Franklin's three youngest children attended high school in Red Bank. Among the varied processes for selecting new teachers at schools in New Jersey, few of them involved parents. They involved school boards and school district bureaucrats, school principals and sometimes teachers, but rarely parents.

Nevertheless, the selection of a new English teacher at his children's high school would be by a panel, on which a parent would be invited to sit along with two existing teachers at the school. Most of the parents available to sit on staff selection panels were mothers, but Americans wanted diversity. Most of the teachers on panels were women, because most of the teachers were women. Thus a few turns of fate and chance brought Franklin to the panel.

Consulting as he was, working from home, Franklin had the time to assist the selection process in normal school hours. The two teachers on the panel weren't about to select a new teacher out of hours.

Children who might have reported much about their teachers to their parents (and about their parents to their teachers) during their first years of school normally had stopped doing so by the time they reached high school, so Franklin asked his children about the two teachers who would sit with him on the panel. Taller than other teachers, although still not as tall as the tallest students, assistant principal Clara Morgenstern was well renowned for enforcing the school rules in a strict and uncompromising manner, as assistant principals did more obviously than anybody else. Franklin's middle son called her scary.

As well as teaching English, Jenny Lowden was co-ordinator of the English as a Second Language program. Slightly built, she often popped up with something she wanted to promote to children who weren't interested. Teachers often did, but she seemed to do so more than most, at least that Franklin's children saw.

The school received thirty-two applications for the English teacher role. While Clara and Jenny received their copies of each application at school, to review there or at their homes, Franklin's youngest daughter collected Franklin's copies in a large envelope from the school office, to bring home to him.

Reviewing those thirty-two applications at home (instead of reading a book from his library that evening), Franklin quickly dismissed most of them. Many of those applicants had submitted such brief applications, it seemed the applicants had little interest in getting the job. Their applications might have been afterthoughts, taking little effort to submit. They might have reflected applicants with so little confidence they would get the job, expending effort on their applications would have been pointless.

Other applicants had expended more time and thought into their applications, but they invoked a sense in Franklin that those applicants simply wanted jobs and income. They would complete the syllabus and promised examination marks to satisfy the parents, but failed to exude the passion for English language and literature that Franklin wanted for his children and other children. Applicants didn't need to match the best of Franklin's teachers decades earlier, but they needed to be closer than most applicants appeared.

Franklin favored the three applications that spoke of rousing children to their literary and other heritage, citing American and other literature. They were Sharyn Bard, Emily Haworth, and Valerie Dickinson.

Thus Monday morning, equipped with their piles of thirty-two printed applications, Franklin met with Clara and Jenny in Clara's modest office at the school. Unlike the suits he wore to business meetings, with or without ties, Franklin dressed down to flannel shirts and trousers, so as not to appear overdressed around the teachers. Their task that day was to decide which applicants they would proceed to interview, and Clara stressed to Franklin that the three of them were equal on the panel: that each of their opinions was of equal value.

"I like Arash Atah," said Clara, more to say that they should proceed to interview him than anything personal.

"Who?" asked Franklin.

"Arash Atah," repeated Clara.

She gave Franklin time to thumb through his copies of the applications to find the one for Arash Atah. He found it, with a cross he'd scribbled in the top right corner because he'd quickly dismissed it upon reading.

"I liked Arash," agreed Jenny, talking about a person she'd never met by his first name, as if they were friends. "I wasn't sure if he was male or she was female," continued Jenny. "The name isn't clear, and I kept looking for a clue in the application."

"He is male," said Franklin, seeing that item in the application form, reading that application more thoroughly than he had the first time. "I must admit," said Franklin, with all the understatement in him, "I was pretty nonplussed about his application."

"I like his whole-of-school initiatives," explained Clara. The focus of Arash's application wasn't anything to do with English or even teaching, but was the anti-racism programs and celebrations of multiculturalism he had orchestrated at the last school at which he'd worked, in Salt Lake City. "We want a teacher who will involve himself in whole-of-school activities."

"I want a teacher who will teach," said Franklin. "As a parent, that's all I'm interested in."

"I wasn't sure if he has taught," added Jenny, without suggesting that was a reason not to interview him. "Do we know if Arash has done any teaching?"

"That was a reason I was nonplussed about him," Franklin elaborated, browsing back through that application. It wasn't the only one.

"He has supported teachers," said Clara, with Arash Atah's application in front of her. "He has developed teaching programs." None of that was actually teaching, thought Franklin. "We can ask his referees if he's been a teacher."

"Don't we want a teacher," asked Franklin, "particularly an English teacher?"

Clara nodded. "That's good you're here to give us that perspective," she said, without Franklin's parental perspective diminishing her enthusiasm to interview Arash. It didn't seem to affect her at all.

"Do you have children at the school?" Franklin asked Clara, in a light tone of voice he hoped sounded convivial.

"I don't have children."

Franklin looked at Jenny. "Do you have children at the school?" he asked her.

"I'm not married."

Clara spoke again. "I also like Phuong Quoc," she said.

"Isn't that a meal?" asked Franklin.

"I also liked Phuong," said Jenny. "Is he a male or she a female?"

Again, Franklin needed to thumb through the applications to find the one Clara liked. Again, this one was marked with a cross that Franklin had scribbled in the top right corner. "Male," Franklin answered Jenny. The application was scant in detail, as several had been, but included that.

"He has teaching experience," said Jenny.

"Teaching English as a second language," read Franklin.

"That's all right."

"For a month," Franklin continued to read, "in Boise, between stints working in a warehouse and a parking lot."

"He has the necessary qualifications and accreditations," said Jenny.

They were the entries under those headings in the application form. "All his qualifications are from Vietnam," said Franklin, reading from the application, "along with an accreditation in Idaho and one in New Jersey in the last six months."

"He meets the criteria," said Clara.

Those criteria can't have been very high, thought Franklin, although he was not a schoolteacher. "I'll defer to you both about qualifications and accreditations," he said, "but are these two the best candidates, from the thirty-two in all?"

"We'll know after we interview them," said Clara.

Reading over his index page listing all the applicants' names, one feature of those two candidates caught Franklin's attention. "Of the thirty-two candidates for this English teaching position," noted Franklin, "these are the only two without American names."

"They are Americans," insisted Clara.

"How do you know they're Americans?" asked Franklin.

"They live here, don't they," replied Clara, as if that were enough.

"Must they be American citizens to teach here?"

"We don't want to be like that," Clara rebuked him, as if Franklin were a student rather than a parent.

There was a lot that Franklin could have said in response, but he had three children at the school and thought better than to say any of it. "I'm always interested in incumbents for any job," said Franklin, moving on. "I don't pay as much attention to what's on paper as to what people who know the incumbent have to say. What do you say about Sharyn Bard?" She taught English at the school in a temporary role.

Jenny looked at Clara. Jenny seemed always to look at Clara, her superior at the school.

"Sharyn does work here," admitted Clara, which was hardly news to Franklin. "I don't know her very well." She turned to Jenny, her underling. "How well do you know Sharyn?"

"I know her," answered Jenny, who was no more revealing to Franklin than Clara had been. "She is competent."

"My son is in her class," said Franklin. "He says she's a good teacher."

Clara didn't look back at her pile of copies of applications for Sharyn's application, as Franklin had done for Arash Atah and Phuong Quoc. "I suppose we should interview Sharyn," admitted Clara.

"We should," said Jenny, as Franklin had learnt to expect Jenny to say in response to anything Clara said. "She is very friendly."

Franklin resumed. "I also thought we should interview Emily Haworth," he said.

"Who?" asked Clara.

"Emily Haworth."

Clara and Jenny looked through their piles of applications. They each, in turn, pulled out their copies of Emily Haworth's application.

"She's already teaching English in New Jersey," explained Franklin, as Clara and Jenny read her application, "in Atlantic Highlands, so she knows the syllabus and this area. She mentioned great literary figures throughout her application: American, British, and German."

Clara was still reading her application. "She doesn't mention any whole-of-school initiatives," said Clara.

"Do you mean anti-racism programs and celebrations of multiculturalism?" asked Franklin.

"For example," answered Clara, although they'd been the only examples she had mentioned.

"Neither had Phuong Quoc," responded Franklin.

"I think we can assume his willingness to be involved."

"Why," asked Franklin, "because he's Vietnamese?"

"He's American," insisted Clara.

"Isn't Emily Haworth?"

"We don't know that."

"We know it more than we know it of Phuong Quoc and Arash Atah," said Franklin.

"How can you say that?"

"All her schooling was in America. If we want to hire the best English teacher for the school, we have more reason to interview Emily Haworth than Phuong Quoc or Arash Atah."

"We can't interview every applicant," said Clara. "I don't want to interview more than three."

"Then let's forget Phuong Quoc and Arash Atah. We need only interview three: Emily Haworth, Sharyn Bard, and Valerie Dickinson."

"Who?" asked Clara.

"Valerie Dickinson," Franklin repeated. "I know most of her teaching is in art, but she exhorts our great poets and she's teaching at another school in Red Bank."

Clara and Jenny looked through their piles of applications, eventually pulling out their copies of Valerie Dickinson's application. "She's more than sixty years of age," read Clara. "Old people aren't very accepting of transgender students and we have two at the school already. We can't hire her."

Franklin hadn't known of any such students at the school. New Jersey law prohibited age discrimination in employment.

Clara put away that application too. "Jenny and I are very keen to interview Phuong Quoc and Arash Atah," she told Franklin. "They are the stand-out candidates."

"They are the...," Franklin started to say, before deciding he shouldn't continue. "All right then," he sighed. "I'll defer to the majority opinion, if we can interview Sharyn Bard too."

The three thus agreed they would interview those three candidates, all of whom were less than thirty years of age. That was about all they had in common.

More than four hours after arriving at the school for that meeting, including telephone calls to confirm, among other things, that Arash Atah had taught a class in Salt Lake City, the meeting concluded. (Such a meeting in the corporations with which Franklin was familiar would have taken fifteen minutes, without any need for telephone calls.)

Franklin, Clara, and Jenny reconvened on Friday morning, around a meeting table in a small meeting room at the school. The blinds over the windows were closed, keeping students and anyone else walking past from seeing inside the room. On the table were printed copies of the questions Clara had suggested, and Jenny and Franklin had agreed, they would ask all three interviewees, with space for notes after each of them. Each candidate would be given the questions ten minutes before their interviews.

On another table stood a jug of water and several glasses, from which Clara set four glasses around the meeting table, including one for the first interviewee. She filled each glass with water.

At nine thirty, according to the schedule Clara had arranged, the first candidate appeared at the open door to be interviewed. Phuong Quoc was gangly, dressed in a modest shirt and trousers, with thin scrappy hair combed almost neatly across his forehead. In his hand was a piece of paper. "Hello," he smiled, in a thick accent Franklin knew must be Vietnamese.

Franklin rose to greet him, as did Clara and Jenny. Clara introduced each of them to Phuong, shaking his hand.

"Hello," said Phuong to each of them.

"Thank you for coming to interview," said Clara, as everyone sat down.

Phuong laid on the table the piece of paper he'd been carrying. He straightened it in front of him, revealing it to be the interview questions he'd been given with handwritten notes after each, in what was presumably Vietnamese.

"I know interviews can be a bit tense," Clara told Phuong, "but please don't be nervous. Have a glass of water and take all the time you need."

"Thank you," answered Phuong, through a voice more Vietnamese accent than English, thought Franklin.

"I will ask the first question," said Clara, holding the paper in front of her. "What skills," she read aloud, "knowledge and expertise do you bring to the position of English teacher at Red Bank?"

Clara, pen in hand, then looked at Phuong. Jenny, pen in hand, also faced Phuong.

Franklin's pen lay on the table. His focus for any interview was the character, manner, and personality of the interviewee. In this case, he wanted to imagine each interviewee teaching English to children in Red Bank, including but not only his children.

Phuong read his notes on the paper in front of him and then talked away. Clara and Jenny wrote notes on their sheets of paper.

Franklin understood few words Phuong said. He leant towards Phuong, turned his head slightly to direct his nearest ear close to him, but still couldn't understand most of what Phuong said. In a pause in Phuong's delivery, Franklin spoke up. "I beg your pardon," said Franklin.

Phuong spoke again, with Carla and Jenny writing notes on their sheets of paper beside the first question. He might have repeated what he'd already said or said something new. Franklin couldn't tell.

In another pause, Franklin again spoke. "Could you please speak a little slower?" he asked.

Phuong smiled. He spoke a little slower. It didn't help Franklin understand him.

Franklin wrote no notes on his sheet of paper; he had nothing to record he could not easily remember. When Phuong appeared to finish, Franklin spoke again. "I'm sorry, Phuong," he said, "I couldn't understand much of what you said."

"We understood," snapped Clara, finishing her long notes in

response to the first question. "Shall we proceed to the next question?" She turned to Jenny. "Would you like to read this one?"

Jenny straightened her piece of paper, also crammed with notes in response to the first question, in front of her. "Talk about an example from your classroom where you were able to successfully design learning so that all students were able to achieve improved outcomes," she read aloud. "How did you do this?"

Again, Phuong read his notes in response to the question. Franklin set himself in his chair, turned his head to align his closest ear again to Phuong, and focused his every thought on deciphering anything he could of Phuong's response. It wasn't much.

When Phuong finished, Franklin again spoke up. "I'm sorry," said Franklin, "I couldn't understand what you said."

"We understood," Clara said again. Phuong smiled.

So it repeated through the remaining three questions. At the end of the interview, twenty or so minutes after it began, they all stood together for the three interviewers to wish Phuong good luck. Clara told him she would revert to him after the panel had selected the new teacher.

After Phuong left, Clara left the room to give the next interviewee, waiting outside in the school offices reception area, his copy of the interview questions. She then returned to the meeting room, closing the door behind her.

"I liked him," said Clara.

"So did I," enthused Jenny.

"How did you understand him?" asked Franklin.

"I got the gist of it," said Clara.

"What gist?" asked Franklin. "How does a man who can hardly speak English teach English to children?"

"He speaks English," insisted Clara. "He can just be a little difficult to understand, sometimes."

"Hello and thank you, he can say," said Franklin. "Beyond that, he might as well have been speaking Vietnamese."

"The students should be exposed to other languages," said Clara.

"Not in their English classes," replied Franklin. "In their English classes, they should be exposed to English."

Almost ten minutes later, Clara brought into the room the next interviewee. Also smiling eagerly at the three of them, Arash Atah appeared uncommonly well dressed for a schoolteacher, thought

Franklin, in a dandy sort of manner. He wore a sparkly bright blue suit with a thin blue tie, which looked like he was about to break into song and dance.

"Good morning," beamed Arash, more clearly than Phuong had spoken. His face and figure were as thin as his suit and tie, and as thin as the hand he offered each interviewer to shake. In Franklin's hand, it lay loose and weak, not really shaking Franklin's hand.

Clara made the same introductions to Arash she'd made to Phuong, with Arash repeatedly cutting across Carla's statements with responses. Unlike Phuong, possibly, Arash admitted to being nervous, jittering about as he did, smiling at Franklin and then Jenny.

Arash placed his hands on the table, visibly collecting himself. He blew a clearing breath.

"No need to be nervous," said Clara, becoming almost motherly to him. "Take a glass of water." He did.

Arash's race wasn't obvious, and none of the three white interviewers dared ask. Franklin thought it was something South Asian, as his name had foreshadowed, but not entirely so.

The notes Arash had written in response to the interview questions, on the piece of paper he set on the table in front of him, appeared to be in English. His handwriting was poor and Franklin only saw it upside down.

Clara embarked upon her five questions, in response to which Arash looked over the words he'd written, before answering. His accent was unmistakable, if not readily identifiable, at least to Franklin, but at least Franklin could understand him. His voice was soft and feminine, lilting in a way that seemed strangely unnatural but also not contrived.

Through the interview, leaning forward onto the table edge, his hands moved around as did his arms and shoulders. Arash spoke repeatedly of his enthusiasm for schools and teaching, proudly speaking of his anti-racism programs and celebrations of multiculturalism he had orchestrated at the last school at which he'd worked, in Salt Lake City. They'd involved every member of what he kept calling the school community.

Calling it a community was a term Clara and Jenny had often also used to describe their school. It was not a term Franklin used to describe the disparate boys and girls who studied and the disparate men and women who taught, parented, and administered there.

Frequently, Arash took glasses of water. Clara assured him, repeatedly, he had no need to be nervous.

Clara invited Franklin to ask Arash the third interview question. "Tell us about an example from your classroom where you used explicit feedback to enhance student learning outcomes," Franklin read aloud, without the words ever sounding like his own.

While his diction sufficed, the jargon and other words Arash spoke made little sense to Franklin. That might have been because Franklin wasn't a schoolteacher, but he didn't think so. He was at least a parent.

The fourth question asked of interviewees let Arash talk of what mattered most to him, and most to Clara and Jenny. "Provide an example," read Clara, "of the impact of your active collaboration within the faculty and across the whole school."

Arash's body rising from his chair and his arms and hands in flight, with all the enthusiasm that Franklin wished Arash felt for teaching English, or teaching any other classroom subject, Arash spoke at length about the anti-racism programs and celebrations of multiculturalism that recurred throughout his answers to the preceding three questions. He desperately wanted to introduce the same into Red Bank.

Clara and Jenny nodded, taking notes as eagerly through this interview as they had through the preceding interview. Time and again, Franklin could have forgotten they were selecting an English teacher.

That interview finished, Arash departed. Clara gave the third interviewee, waiting in the school offices reception area, her sheet of paper with the five questions, before again returning to the meeting room and closing the door behind her. "I like him," enthused Clara, with longer pronunciation and almost a song in her voice, as she sat back at the table. "He was nervous, but I like him."

"So do I," said Jenny. She hadn't needed to say so, thought Franklin.

"He never spoke of English teaching," said Franklin. "It was all everything outside the classroom, along with how much he wanted the job. There was nothing for the students, but the job he wanted for himself."

"I didn't get that," said Clara. Jenny said much the same as Clara said, again.

Finally, the third candidate interviewed was Sharyn Bard. Her blouse and skirt were at the better end of schoolmistress clothes, but still schoolmistress clothes. Her smile was more relaxed than the preceding two interviewees' smiles had been, as it might because she already taught at the school and already knew Clara and Jenny.

Sharyn spoke less of her enthusiasm for schools, but spoke instead of novels, plays, and poetry, including Chaucer and Shakespeare. What struck Franklin most about her was that her words sounded like those of an English teacher, as Arash's words had not. He still had no idea what Phuong had said.

Franklin imagined Sharyn, but not Phuong or Arash, teaching English in front of a class of children at the school. He couldn't imagine Phuong or Arash teaching anything.

After the same four questions asked of all interviewees, Clara asked the same fifth and final question. "Do you have anything else to add?"

Repeating the words of her application, as Arash had done and Phuong might have done, Sharyn spoke of editing the most recent edition of the school magazine. She spoke of her final-year students achieving marks well above average, and indeed the best marks at the school.

After the three interviews, with two of the three candidates gone elsewhere, Sharyn returned to her classroom. Seated around the table in the meeting room, with the door closed and no one else to see, Clara, Jenny, and Franklin discussed the three interviewees.

"I like Arash," Clara said again.

"He's not an English teacher," insisted Franklin. "We're not appointing an anti-racism officer or convener for celebrations of multiculturalism," he elaborated, presuming from his children's time at the school it had already appointed one of each, or several. "We're appointing an English teacher."

"Arash can teach English," said Clara.

"How can you know?" asked Franklin. "He never sounded like an English teacher, in his written application or in the interview. I'm not expecting we'll find Miss Jean Brodie, but this one's closer to a hat stand."

"Ooh," said Clara, leaning back in her chair. "I don't think that."

"Neither do I," said Jenny.

Franklin continued to plead. "I want a teacher to speak of great literature," he said. "I want a teacher to inspire the children to read. Has he heard of Shakespeare, or Chaucer?"

"He will have heard of some writers," answered Clara, presuming a lot, thought Franklin. "They might not be writers we know."

"He never mentioned any writers," continued Franklin. "He never mentioned anyone, but himself."

"For many of our students," said Clara, "their heritage isn't American. Arash can inspire all the students to other literature."

Franklin imagined Clara edging towards a description of that literature reflecting Arash's race, but however much race appeared to draw Clara and Jenny to Phuong and Arash, neither one admitted it. Franklin wasn't brave enough to mention it, not with children at the school or even, he realized, if he didn't have children at the school.

That literature Franklin wanted children to love wasn't just American but was also English, Irish, Scottish, Welsh, and other European, as Franklin hadn't previously appreciated. It wasn't from wherever Arash Atah's forebears came.

Wanting a teacher to inspire children to their heritage was racist, when the children were white. Wanting to inspire children of other races to their heritage would be just as racist, but nobody worried about that.

Wanting to inspire children, whatever their race, in American schools to America's cultural heritage was also racist, because America's cultural heritage was a pan-European heritage. The cultural heritage of other races was just as racist, but nobody worried about that.

What remained without race wasn't culture. It wasn't literature or any other arts. It was anti-racism programs and celebrations of multiculturalism.

"We want the children to be worldly," insisted Clara. "We need teachers supporting whole-of-school activities."

Jenny echoed her. "We need teachers supporting faculty initiatives," said Jenny. Like whole-of-school activities, faculty initiatives didn't mean teaching English in a classroom. It meant anti-racism programs and celebrations of multiculturalism.

"Sharyn compiled and edited the last school magazine," Franklin pointed out, of a task with some connection to teaching English. "People say she did very well, organizing different people, bringing everything together ahead of time and budget."

"She did," admitted Clara. She could hardly not.

"That's a whole-of-school activity," Franklin elaborated, a little embarrassed if only to himself to use a term that had become so hackneyed in his hearing that week, and that he had never before used and would never use again. "It's a faculty initiative."

Clara was slow to respond. Her voice doing so was just as slow. "The school magazine is a whole-of-school activity," she admitted, although it plainly wasn't a whole-of-school activity she had in mind. "It isn't really a faculty initiative."

"It isn't," agreed Jenny, and it was her faculty in question.

"In my experience," said Franklin, more of corporations than schools, "people taking on these optional extras like anti-racism programs and celebrations of multiculturalism aren't any more dedicated than those who don't. They're single people without families to entertain them, or to tend to."

"Ooh," said Clara sitting back. So did Jenny.

"I can understand," said Franklin, "all else being equal, favoring someone engaged in whole-of-school activities, but these candidates aren't equal. They're not even close to being equal. If we had no other applicants, I still wouldn't hire Arash. I'd call again for applications."

Clara reached forward in her chair towards Franklin, in the sense she would impart something confidential to him. "I know we're not supposed to think like this," she said, "but we want more male teachers to be role models for the boys. Many of them don't have any adult males at home."

Franklin almost laughed. "I don't think Arash is a role model for boys," he responded.

Clara took more time to speak than she normally did. "Do you feel that because...," she started to say, slowly choosing her best words, "he's effeminate?"

"No," replied Franklin, because he felt he had to say that. "He has the manner of a boy, without any gravitas of a man. The boys would see him as one of them."

Those last words weren't strictly sincere. They were the best that Franklin felt free to say, in a country that wanted male role models without masculinity, because it wanted men without masculinity.

Still, that was an encouraging moment of candor from Clara about gender driving her thinking, and so Jenny's thinking, that there wasn't about race. Clara and Jenny hadn't suggested interviewing any of the male Americans among those thirty-two initial applicants, few of them as there were.

In that meeting room behind a closed door and blinds, the three supposedly equal members of the staff selection panel talked and talked, but nothing changed. At some point, Franklin realized that Clara had long decided to hire Arash and that Jenny agreed. Whether Jenny agreed with Clara because she agreed with everything that her superior at the school said or because they were both products of the same environment wasn't for Franklin to determine.

In submission, four and a half hours after he'd arrived there that morning, Franklin raised his hands and opened his palms to the air. "You are the majority," he acknowledged. The school would offer the job of teaching English to Arash Atah.

Unlike Clara and Jenny, Franklin wasn't paid to be there. His work (as well as his library) awaited him at home, to which his three youngest children would return at the end of their school day.

Franklin stood up from his chair, preparing to leave. "The purpose of involving parents in school decisions isn't to influence decisions that schools make, is it?" he said to them.

Clara and Jenny in their chairs sat looking up at him. There was none of the formalities of Franklin's departure afforded the three interviewees.

"It's the same purpose of most consultation we see nowadays," continued Franklin, "isn't it? It's to deceive us into thinking we influence decisions. It's to validate the decisions you make without us, to validate the invalid." Franklin never again sat on a staff selection panel.

8 TEACHING

College degrees often encouraged graduates to feel knowledgeable, even expert, in their fields. Suzie O'Meara did, after completing her college education majoring in American history in Omaha, where she'd grown up with her family. Soon after graduating, she moved with her boyfriend to Baltimore, after he took a job there. With her qualifications and accreditations in place, Suzie was ready to be a schoolteacher in Maryland much as she'd once planned to be a schoolteacher in Nebraska, imparting all she could of that knowledge she'd accumulated.

Her life had always felt predictable. Suzie liked it that way.

Many jobs for young people, and older people, had become temporary, as was the job on offer teaching American history at a Baltimore high school, while the usual teacher's leave extended through Spring Break into the new term. The school's promotional literature spoke of the school's academic excellence, social harmony, and safety. If it seemed to imply other schools were not so excellent, harmonious, or safe, Suzie felt certain that was not the intention.

Deliberating about whether to dress for her job interview in her best clothes or in the ordinary nice clothes she expected teachers to wear, Suzie opted for the latter. She wanted her interviewer to see a teacher, not an interviewee.

Suzie felt certain her clothes should be close to those that children wore, but not too close. She needed to appear older than the children were to ensure their respect (she was only twenty-three years of age) but not so much older as to seem distant from them. Her pale brown hair was neither as long as young girls wore it nor as short as older women wore it, but was the betwixt and between length that Suzie felt in herself at that time in life.

Across Suzie's nose and cheeks were several soft freckles, which her boyfriend said were cute but that Suzie feared made her appear younger than she was. The time in life would come that she would be glad for anything that made her appear younger than she was, her mother had often told her, but she'd not yet reached that time. She covered her freckles, as best she could, with powder.

In spite of it being Spring Break, litter lay scattered about the open areas of the school when Suzie arrived there for her interview. There was also more concrete and fewer trees than at the Nebraskan schools in which she had been a pupil, which seemed more years ago than it really was. It was only five years.

Interviewing Suzie in his office was the school's assistant principal, Herbert Underwood, a man as old as Suzie's father but more tired in his manner and more gray in his appearance. His long gray sideburns only advertised his age.

Wearing his dusty sports jacket as he stood in front of her, his eyes ran over Suzie's comfortable pale blouse, blue denim jacket, and long blue denim dress, covering most of her long leather boots (which made her a little taller, where every bit of height might help). "That's good," he told her. "You want to dress better than the students so they respect you, but not so well as to give an impression you think you're better than they are."

Whether she should feel slighted, Suzie wasn't sure. At least he approved.

Herbert motioned Suzie towards the empty chair in front of his desk. She sat where he'd directed her, while he sat in his chair behind his desk, cluttered with papers overlapping each other and with an antiquated computer screen to one side. "You should know," said Herbert, "that most children at this school are underprivileged. They're good kids, but they haven't had the privileges you and I have had. You need to leave them some slack."

Suzie nodded. "I understand," she said.

"I know you do," smiled Herbert. "We are particularly proud at this school to be minority majority."

"I find the diversity in Baltimore interesting," said Suzie, before realizing she should convey her enthusiasm. "I find it exciting."

"So do we," he grinned.

The interview continued with questions about Suzie's past in Omaha and her future plans in Baltimore. In short, she'd always wanted to be a schoolteacher, never wanted to be anything else, studying American history in college only to become one. She loved children, loved teaching, and loved American history. She expected to remain in Baltimore indefinitely.

Herbert's lips closed, his teeth appeared to chew while Suzie spoke, although there was no food in his mouth that Suzie saw. It might have been his habit while he thought, or might have just been his habit. She couldn't let it be off-putting.

When Suzie finished, whatever she'd said had been enough for Herbert to stand up, smile, and walk around his desk towards her. "Welcome to our school community," he told her.

"Thank you," smiled Suzie, also standing up, wanting to reach out and hug him.

Instead, Herbert reached out his hand to shake hers. She took it and shook it, more eagerly than he did. He laughed. "I think you'll fit in swell here," he told her. "I'll make sure you know when the next permanent history teaching position becomes available."

Her employment, albeit temporary, gave Suzie the confidence to buy more blouses, skirts, and even another denim jacket, different to the one she already owned; Baltimore was warmer than Omaha had been, making her thickest coat and jumpers superfluous but not denying her the need of a jacket, or two. No item of her clothing replicated another, so no girl in the class could suspect her of wearing the same clothes too often, as she'd suspected of some of her teachers at school.

The first day of the new term, Suzie dressed much as she'd dressed for her interview, but in clothes deliberately different to those she'd worn to her interview, even if Herbert Underwood would be the only person to know it. Among her preparations and introductions she'd rehearsed in conversation with her boyfriend, the easiest to implement was advice she'd long ago been given. She would not tell the children that this was her first day teaching, whereby she would lose all authority. Eventually, some weeks or months later when she had proven her expertise, she could mention it.

Suzie hung her handbag over her shoulder. In her hand, she brought her book of George Washington's writings. Bought from the bookstore in the old Baltimore power plant, the book was her treat to herself for getting a job. It would also be her means to inspire her students.

At the school, dressed as he'd dressed when Suzie last saw him, Herbert Underwood led Suzie to the open door of the classroom in which she would lead her classes. Over her shoulder, her handbag hung. In her hand, she carried her book.

"Normally," said Herbert, "I'd come in and introduce you to

the students, but I have a small emergency to deal with. This class is above the average academically; you won't need me." He left her there.

Through the open door, Suzie stepped. A handful of books, papers, and pens lay on scattered table desks. A handful of teenaged boys and girls sat at scattered table desks, but not the same table desks as those on which the books, papers, and pens lay. The rest of the boys and girls stood in small groups at those desks or away from desks altogether, amidst conversations and laughing, without noticing the stranger at the door.

Suzie understood the children could be restless their first day back from a break. She proceeded to the large teacher's desk at the front of the classroom, on which she stood her handbag and rested her book. Around the classroom walls were posters like those she was accustomed to seeing in school classrooms, although a few posters hung loosely or were torn.

Behind her teacher's desk, Suzie stood before her first class. Few children were white. Most were black or Latino. The groups in which they'd sat and stood were their own: the few white children together, several groups all black, several groups Latino.

Most boys wore hooded jackets, some with hoods over their heads and some hanging open behind their necks. Most girls wore loosely hanging pale linen shirts, along with denim jeans tighter than those the boys wore. Boys and girls wore their black hair in a variety of styles Suzie hadn't realized hair could have. Some boys sprouted moustaches and the first hairs of beards.

Suzie's denim jacket and skirt remained blue as none of the denim the students wore remained. She felt she'd dressed appropriately.

Suzie counted twenty-three boys and girls. She returned to the classroom door, closed it, and felt from that moment the classroom was hers.

Trying to speak above the boys and girls, Suzie drew upon her firmest voice. "Good morning," she said, as she walked back to her teacher's desk at the front of the classroom.

None of the boys or girls responded. They continued talking, laughing, and listening among their groups, including those few boys and girls looking generally towards her.

Suzie stood again behind her teacher's desk, facing her first class. Shouting would seem like she couldn't control the class, and

Suzie never shouted, but she nevertheless raised her voice without shouting. "Good morning," she said again. "Can everyone please sit down?"

Again, none of them, not even the handful facing her, responded. They continued talking and laughing among their groups. The voice from other teachers that had stilled classes in Omaha in which Suzie once sat wasn't stilling that class in Baltimore.

Suzie raised her voice further, still without shouting. "Mister Ayres remains on leave," she tried to tell them. "I am Miss O'Meara. I will be your relief teacher until Mister Ayres is well again."

Amidst the continuing conversations and laughing, Suzie heard one girl facing her tell the other girls at her desk: "Ayres is sick."

They laughed. "Was it us?" one asked. They laughed again.

Suzie took her book lying on her teacher's desk in her hands. Holding two of its corners with both her hands, she raised the book above her head. Bracing herself, but not knowing what else to do, she crashed the book against the desk.

The thud shook the desk, the room, and Suzie. The two dozen voices and laughter stopped in an instant, as every boy and girl faced Suzie.

Her voice returned to normal. "Mister Ayres is still on leave," repeated Suzie. "I am Miss O'Meara. I will be your relief teacher until Mister Ayres is well again. Please, take your seats."

The girls at first and then the boys moved slowly towards their chairs. They sat down, some with a murmur between themselves that Suzie thought better to ignore.

When only the slowest straggling boys had not yet sat, but without letting them delay her or the class, Suzie spoke again, with the words she had spent days preparing. "I've been thinking of excursions we can take in Baltimore to see American history," she told them.

"This class don't do excursions," one boy replied from his desk.

"Shuddup, ant brain," another boy told him.

That was enough of a reprimand for Suzie not to add one of her own. "Fells Point is historical," she told them. "So is Fort McHenry. My boyfriend likes…"

"You have a boyfriend?" asked one boy.

The girl at the desk beside him reached closer to him. She

jabbed her elbow at his side.

"Hey," he cried out, grabbing his side where she'd jabbed him.

Suzie resumed. "My boyfriend likes baseball more than I do," she said, "but he took me to the house where Babe Ruth was born; it's now a museum. You boys might like that. The girls might too."

"I hate baseball," said one boy, at the back of the room. "It's American."

"Aren't you American?" Suzie asked him.

"Do I look American?"

Suzie stared at the boy (she had to believe he was a boy, in spite of his moustache and beard starting to sprout), as a few of the voices around the room began to snigger. "You sound American," she told him.

Some in the class laughed. Suzie didn't know at whom.

"I'm Puerto Rican," he told her, "and I look Puerto Rican."

If the laughter subsided, it didn't subside very much. "I am sorry," said Suzie. "I didn't detect your accent."

The laughter rose again. "I don't need an accent to be Puerto Rican," he told her. "Do Africans need accents to be Africans? Do Mexicans need accents to be Mexican?"

"No," agreed Suzie. "Of course you don't. Of course they don't."

"Good."

The laughter slowly subsided, clearly this time. If Suzie passed that test, it was only just. "Were you born in San Juan?" she asked him, demonstrating her knowledge of Puerto Rico.

"I was born in Baltimore," he countered. "You gonna ask me my life story?"

The laughter rose again, more than ever. The boy sitting next to the Puerto Rican boy reached out his clenched fist and the Puerto Rican boy clenched his, thumping the two fists together. They might both have been Puerto Rican.

Suzie waited for them to put away their fists and the laughter to die down, before resuming. "I was thinking I'd approach the school about taking you all on an excursion," she told the class. "Have any of you visited the Star-Spangled Banner Flag House? I have. It was great."

"If we don't want to see baseball," the Puerto Rican told her, "then we won't want to see the Star-Spackled Banner, will we?"

"Star-Spangled Banner," Suzie corrected him; she felt teachers should correct errors from their pupils. "Other boys and girls might like to see it, and you might find you like it more than you expect."

"I won't like it," he told her. "None of the Puerto Ricans will. The Mexicans won't. The Africans won't."

Suzie looked around the room. She hadn't dwelt upon the nationality or race of anybody there; she didn't want to start. She turned back to the Puerto Rican. "May I please know your name?" she asked him.

He leant back in his chair. "Juan," he answered. The class again laughed. "San Juan," he smiled. The class laughed louder still; he was plainly no saint.

Suzie could neither be seen to believe him nor be seen not to believe him, as the laughter slowly abated. Smiles remained on the children's faces as if to say they expected to be laughing again soon; the children didn't seem to tire of laughing, at least in Suzie's class that morning. "Would you like to see the maritime museum?" Suzie asked him. "You can visit an old boat."

Another boy in the class responded. "It beats schoolwork," he said.

More boys and girls laughed, but Juan (for the want of another name) bellowed over them: "No!"

That second boy stood from his chair, facing Juan. "My cousin's navy," said the boy. "I want to go."

"Thank…" Suzie started to say.

"My cousins aren't navy," Juan cut across her, standing from his chair and facing the other boy.

"Both of you," commanded Suzie, with a depth in her voice she hadn't before known, "sit down!"

Both boys remained standing, facing each other. A murmur moved around the room.

"There'll be no excursions," said Suzie, "if you both don't sit down."

"Good," said Juan.

"We could go without you," Suzie threatened.

"Woah!" called out another boy. More boys and girls laughed, but not Juan.

He stared at Suzie, as Suzie stared at him, while boys and girls laughed and spoke between themselves. The other boy slowly sat down.

Over the top of the sounds other children made, Juan addressed Suzie. "Didn't anyone tell you not to mess with the Puerto Ricans?"

Suzie braced herself, holding her stare at the boy. "I don't see nationality," she told him.

"You better learn to see it, if you want to survive, Whitey."

Boys and girls laughed, as Juan looked around at them. He laughed with them as if they were his, not Suzie's, audience.

Suzie stood firm, staring back at Juan. "I don't see myself as being white," she insisted. "I don't see race."

Juan laughed. Other boys and girls laughed louder.

Suzie drew upon her firmest voice. "The only race is the human race."

Juan laughed louder. It seemed all the boys and girls laughed loudly, but not the white children at the side of the classroom. They sat somberly and still.

"I'm American," insisted Suzie.

"And this guy?" asked Juan, pointing at the boy who'd previously stood, whose cousin was in the navy.

That boy edged from his seat towards Juan. Suzie thought the boy might stand. He didn't.

"Isn't he black?" asked Juan. "Isn't he African?"

That other boy laughed, as everybody laughed, but Suzie. She kept her eyes on Juan. "I hadn't noticed," she said.

"Hey!" said the other boy, standing up and facing Suzie. "Whaddya mean by that?"

Suzie faced him. "I see only a classroom of students," she tried to assure him.

The girl sitting beside the boy moved closer to him, edging higher from her chair. She too was black; Suzie chastised herself for noticing. "Forget it," the girl told the boy. "I want to go on excursions."

He looked back at the girl. She glared at him, as he slowly sat back in his chair.

Juan had become momentarily incidental to the drama played out around him, but he'd remained standing throughout it. As Suzie turned back to face him, he turned back to face her. "I ain't going to any maritime museum," he told her.

"I know," she responded, somewhat pleased with herself that she did.

He continued staring at her. If he was trying to think of a retort, it came slowly to him.

"Please," Suzie told him, toying with calling him Juan with a smile, "sit down."

A long conceited grin crept through his face. He began shaking his head.

"I said please," continued Suzie, "sit down."

That smile slowly left his face, as he reached his right hand behind his back. "What did I tell you about messing with Puerto Ricans?" he asked her.

"I told you," said Suzie, as the boy slowly brought back his right hand from behind him, "I don't see…"

In the boy's hand was a knife. Somebody gasped.

Suzie froze. Her eyes fixed on that knife, slowly pointing towards her, before her eyes slowly returned to him.

Juan stepped away from his chair, into the aisle between desks. He didn't need to watch the knife to know how to use it, Suzie knew. His searing eyes, unafraid at least of her, remained set upon her eyes, stabbing her as surely as that knife threatened to stab her.

"Now, Whitey," said Juan, "why don't you think up an excursion we all want to take?"

Other boys, some girls as well, started to laugh. They laughed loudly, as if demanding that Suzie hear them laugh.

Suzie stepped back, turned, and moved towards the closed classroom door. The children laughed louder, one hollered, which made more children laugh even louder, as Suzie opened the door and rushed out.

She hurried along the corridor, her pace quickening still further, as every closed door she neared became threatening. Down the stairs she rushed to ground level and out of the building, along her way to the administrative offices. The people loitering around the open areas of the school weren't worth approaching.

Suzie rushed through the administrative reception area to the assistant principal's office at which she'd been interviewed. The office door was open. The office was empty.

She ran to the nearby principal's office. That door was partly open, whereby Suzie pushed it completely open.

In front of her, sitting at his desk conspicuously clean and empty, must have been the school principal, wearing a dusty sports jacket that could have come from Herbert Underwood's wardrobe.

Covering the principal's face was a gray beard that could have been the facial hair Herbert Underwood aspired to wear. Sitting in the chair facing him, wearing another sports jacket, was Herbert Underwood.

"It's hell there," cried Suzie, ready to weep. She crashed into an empty chair also facing the principal's desk.

The principal looked at Herbert, who responded. "Suzie O'Meara is teaching history temporarily," explained Herbert, "while Timothy Ayres is on leave."

From his desk, the principal nodded. That might have been the signal for Herbert to rise from his chair.

Suzie turned to watch Herbert cross the floor, close the door, and return to his chair beside her. "Suzie," he said, "this is our principal, Lyle Faulkner."

Even seated at his chair at his desk, Lyle Faulkner was obviously tall. Wherever his beard didn't cover it, his face was gaunt but relaxed, like a man ready to retire. "Is this your first day teaching, Suzie?" asked Lyle, his voice almost paternal. "I think most of us found our first day teaching stressful."

"This isn't stress," replied Suzie. "It's mortal combat."

Lyle's voice remained calm. "You are being melodramatic," he told her.

"A student pulled a knife on me."

Lyle looked at Herbert. "Investigate will you?" he asked. "You know the protocols."

Herbert stepped quickly away, opened the door, and departed. He left the door open.

Lyle rose from his chair, walked across his office, and closed the door. "What happened, Suzie?" he asked her, walking back to his desk and chair.

"I've just had a Puerto Rican…"

"We don't refer to people by their background," said Lyle, sitting back down.

"This boy did."

Lyle clasped his hands together on his desk. "Does this boy have a name, Suzie?" he inquired.

"I asked him and he said he was Juan, San Juan, but he was obviously lying."

"You might have upset him by asking his name, Suzie. A lot of children are very sensitive."

"He's not sensitive," insisted Suzie. "He's brutal!"

Lyle sighed. "Juan isn't brutal," he replied, his voice and manner unwaveringly calm. "He's a child."

"I'm not sure he is a child," said Suzie, not entirely joking. "Would we know if he's a man impersonating a child?"

"He's sensitive," insisted Lyle, unperturbed by anything Suzie said. "Have you forgotten what you were like as a child?"

"I was never like this."

"I'm sure the boys in your class were."

"They weren't," said Suzie. "They could be rough with each other and sometimes mean to girls, when we were little, but never anything like this, and never anything like this to a teacher."

Lyle shook his head. "Now, now," he told her. "I think you've forgotten your school days."

"You've forgotten yours," responded Suzie, "and failed to grasp how far removed your school was from the jungle you've got here."

"Please don't use words with racial connotations, Suzie."

She laughed. "The kids talk race and you worry about connotations," she told him.

"We have no racial conflict here," insisted Lyle.

"The blacks and Puerto Ricans...."

"They're teasing you, Suzie," Lyle told her, "seeing how you react, and you failed. When children tell me we have racial tension, I tell them I don't believe them. I tell them we have only racial harmony and I say so repeatedly. They soon learn that I won't give them the distress they want in me. They soon stop saying it."

Suzie sat staring at him. That small closed office in which they sat was a world away from the classroom in which she'd stood.

"The white children are the worst," continued Lyle, "the boys and the girls. They'll tell you they're being bullied by one ethnic group or another for being white, but I tell them I won't tolerate their lying. They eventually stop."

Suzie sat remembering the races of children in her class. The white children had been quiet.

"Tell me precisely what happened, Suzie," said Lyle.

She slowly collected her breath. "I wanted to inspire the boys and girls to learn about history," Suzie told him, "so I suggested speaking to someone about taking them on an excursion."

Lyle shook his head. "This school doesn't encourage

excursions," he told her.

"I thought I could take them to Fells Point, Fort McHenry…"

"That won't interest them," Lyle interrupted.

"I'm trying to teach them American history."

Lyle slowly nodded. "Try to think more broadly about American history, Suzie," he suggested.

"What does that mean?"

"Try to think of American history they consider their own."

"I thought they owned all of it," replied Suzie. "I wanted to show them the Babe Ruth Museum and Star-Spangled Banner Flag House."

"You didn't?" said Lyle, shaking his head. "We need to get you some diversity training."

Suzie thought carefully before responding. "Do you want me to tailor my teaching to the children's race?" she asked him.

"I want you to be sensitive."

She nodded. "Then you want me to say whatever immigrant children want to hear without admitting it," she said, "whatever that means for American sensitivities: the white boys and girls?"

"What we have been doing here," Lyle assured her, "and at other schools in Baltimore, has been very successful."

"We can't please them all," lamented Suzie. "That's diversity."

"Other teachers have."

"By not pleasing anyone?"

Lyle sat staring at her, before slowly speaking. "I've been pleased."

When she'd tired of looking back at him, Suzie's eyes left him to look around his office. Around the walls were photographs of Lyle with people Suzie didn't recognize, along with certificates of appreciation from clubs and associations she didn't know. They made his office look busy, as his empty desk did not. His computer screen was probably newer than any other she'd seen at the school, but not by much.

"Suzie," Lyle resumed, drawing her attention back to him, "are you sure you're mature enough to be a teacher?"

His words were a coded means of telling her she wasn't. "There's a constant racial tension through this school," she informed him. "We're never more than a wrong word or look away from a knife being drawn against us."

Lyle shook his head, glancing at the clock at the side of his desk.

"You have been at this school for less an hour, Suzie," he told her. "I have been teaching here and at other schools in Baltimore since before you were born."

"When did you last leave your office?" Suzie asked him. "I suspect I've spent more time teaching these past ten years than you have."

A man engaged in his work might have been offended with her response, thought Suzie. "I keep in touch," he replied.

"You don't believe children telling you there are problems," she pressed him, "so they give up telling you. When did parents give up telling you?"

Lyle motioned his slow arm and hand towards the door behind her. "My door is always open," he told her, "as you found when you came here."

"It's closed now."

"I've closed it for you," he replied, slowly pulling back his arm and hand. "We are very proud of our diversity."

Suzie laughed. "I know," she told him. "You're too proud to pay attention to people who would dent your delusions of greatness."

A loud knock came through the closed door. "Herbert?" Lyle called out.

The door opened, revealing Herbert Underwood. In one hand, he carried Suzie's handbag (carrying it by the bag, not the handle, as men did carrying women's handbags) and her book she had left behind in the classroom. He closed the door behind him. "There was no knife," he told Lyle.

"I saw it," insisted Suzie.

Presumably meaning Suzie to hear, Herbert continued addressing Lyle. "The children are reviewing their past work while we find someone else to teach them," said Herbert.

He gave Suzie her handbag and book. She rested them on her lap.

Herbert then sat back in the chair in which he'd been sitting when Suzie first entered that office. "I have spoken to several students," continued Herbert, addressing Suzie loud enough for Lyle to hear, "including the boy who said he was standing addressing you when you ran out. He said he raised his hand to make a point without realizing he was still holding his pen and is sorry it frightened you, but he showed me the pen and I can see why you thought it was a knife."

"I know a knife," insisted Suzie. "Do you think I eat my meals with a pen and fork?"

"Other students confirmed it was only the pen."

"Were those students Puerto Ricans too?" asked Suzie. "Did you ask the black students? Did you ask the white students? I don't know what to make of the Mexican students." Whether the Puerto Ricans mixed with the Mexicans, she couldn't tell. She couldn't distinguish them.

"I wasn't grouping them," said Herbert. "Neither should you."

"They group themselves."

"Suzie," Lyle interjected. "You're supposed to be a teacher? You're supposed to be intellectual?"

She turned to face him. "Isn't confronting the reality of race intellectual?"

"That's pseudo-intellectualism," said Lyle, sounding like the worst of students Suzie had encountered at college.

Suzie shook her head, taking refuge by looking down at her lap, handbag, and book. From the front cover of her book looking up at her was a portrait of George Washington, who could never have imagined the eventual decline of the country he'd fought to create and defend. "What you call pseudo-intellectualism," said Suzie, "is the intellectualism you don't want to hear."

"Please…," said Lyle.

"You wouldn't understand," Suzie told them, looking up again at Lyle, "you're white."

"Aren't you?"

Suzie stared back into his blue-green eyes: his white person's eyes, as hers were. "Yes," she said. "I am white."

"We are privileged."

Suzie shook her head. "We're not privileged," she said. "We're ignorant."

Lyle sighed. "Would you like to go home now, Suzie?" he asked her.

"Why is Timothy Ayres on sick leave?"

"You will appreciate we have privacy issues, Suzie."

"Is he suffering stress, acute stress?"

"Timothy is a very popular staff member," said Lyle. "He is a very popular teacher."

"Did that help him?"

"I think you should go home, Suzie," Lyle repeated. "Mister Underwood can find us another, more mature, relief teacher."

"I can teach," said Suzie, "but teaching requires knowledge to begin with. I am white, confronting boys and girls many of whom are not and they know they are not, better than you both know and better than I knew when I arrived here this morning. They haven't forgotten what they are and what we are because we've stopped paying attention."

Suzie pulled her handbag back onto her shoulder and took her book back in her hand. She stood up from her chair, looking down at Lyle and Herbert still sitting in theirs, looking up at her.

"I'll go back to my classroom," Suzie told them, whatever the two old men in the dusty sports jackets thought of that. "I'm going to teach the history I love to teach and that makes me proud to be American, and if the only students I inspire to love this country are the white ones then I'll be satisfied with that. This is America, and the other boys and girls are going to have to hear American history in an American history class I teach. They're going to have to learn American history if they're going to get good grades from me, whatever and whoever they like and dislike, including me. You can call this morning my diversity training."

"Suzie," Lyle stopped her, "no."

9 CONGRESS

After Western countries opened their borders, white populations declined, their power dissolved, and their cultures disbanded. None of that dissuaded them from their course. It only encouraged them in it, determined to court favor from immigrant populations who demanded respect for their own that white people no longer expected. Nobody courted their favor more than politicians, and no politician more so than Logan Bates.

Representing his congressional district in Florida, Logan had fattened over the years but, being as tall as he was, carried his weight with the authority of incumbency. When he needed to appear erudite, he wore his spectacles, although his eyesight had always been limited and he should have worn spectacles since he was young.

His whitening hair, which once connoted authority in a person, no longer did, not in America. Most people who rarely saw Logan probably didn't notice his hair slowly darkening. (The journalists who didn't ask about it were probably unwilling to draw attention to their dyed hair.) Among his longstanding Floridian supporters and donors close enough to notice were members of the Ingram family, seeing him as often as they did at fundraising events in their home. To be exact, Mrs. Ingram noticed, but hers was the sort of family in which parents and children spoke freely, if only with each other.

Representing the Democratic Party had stopped being enough to guarantee Logan's re-election, even after almost six terms in Congress. For the first time in years, Logan was challenged in the Democratic Party primaries, as other Congressmen and women around America were challenged. His challenger was a young Hispanic woman whose only qualification for the role might have been that she was Hispanic, but that would probably be enough for his increasingly Hispanic district.

Logan answered his challenger's charge that he had tinted his white skin darker in his campaign photographs by saying his campaign staff simply corrected over-exposure by the camera. The Florida sun explained his darkening skin, Logan added, although he'd spent more time in cold Washington than warm Florida those past twelve years.

The Congressman had also learnt to speak Spanish, to say a few words to audiences warming to him because he did. Immigration was a blessing for America, he declared, to cheers from immigrants and college students, if not from older Americans and those no longer able to enter college. The specific immigration he called a blessing depended upon his audience, but most of the time was that from somewhere to the south. The more Logan spoke of hope and optimism for a future with fewer white Americans, the more immigrants and college students liked him.

Conversely, the more Logan spoke of fear and pessimism for the future because of prejudice and corporate power, the more those immigrants and college students liked him. The more he spoke of fear for the future due to rising carbon levels in the Earth's atmosphere, college students liked him even more.

Together, those hopes and fears earned Logan the Democratic Party nomination to his district again. Against his Hispanic challenger, they did so narrowly.

Whenever his Republican Party opponent in the general election spoke to fear about immigration or against fear about everything else, the more Logan attacked him for his negativity or for his lack of negativity. Logan attacked him for being an aging white male, as if Logan's love for immigration exempted him from also being an aging white male.

Thus the voters in his district returned Logan to Washington for a seventh Congressional term. He had proved his usefulness.

No voters were more enthusiastic for Logan, or more generous in their donations and donations they procured, than the Ingram family. That generosity, more than that enthusiasm, brought their eldest son Daryl to Washington to be an unpaid intern, at the start of Logan's seventh term. Having completed his college education and then vacationing in Europe, Daryl's parents continued supporting him, accommodating him in the old Hotel Lombardy along Pennsylvania Avenue until he found an apartment he liked.

Daryl had always kept himself well groomed, his hair short and naturally parted, and worn smart casual clothes nicer than some suits some people wore, so he needed little preparation for his internship. His suits he'd brought with him from home, along with a heavy woolen hat and coat that had been harder to find in Florida.

After the grandeur of the public areas of Congress, through which Daryl again walked his first Sunday afternoon in Washington, and even the House of Representatives lobby in which he waited Monday morning, the private offices section was a little underwhelming. Corridors were shining clean and long, with occasional paintings on the walls, but nothing like the art that tourists saw. Marking each Congressman or woman's door from the corridor were American and state flags that no one paused to notice, although some stopped at the small desks against the wall.

Only the clothes were better among the offices, with men in suits and women wearing red, blue, and darker colors. Tourists in their public areas wore the casual clothes of brighter colors Daryl had worn one day earlier, even if they normally weren't as good as Daryl's clothes.

The nicest spaces were each Congressman or woman's offices, with the mammoth seal of the House of Representatives shining from Logan's carpet. Among the paintings, photographs, and other gifts cluttering Logan's offices, Daryl recognized only some of the pictured places and people from home with whom smiling Logan posed. The largest of Logan's framed photographs was of him smiling with former president Barack Obama.

Late in his first morning, after the inductions and introductions, the man Daryl found in his private office was unlike the man in those photographs or the man he'd so often admired at home in Florida. In a building where there seemed an inordinate number of dark leather buttoned cushioned sofas, Logan sat slumped in another one. He wore a suit so crumpled a stranger might not realize how good a suit it was. With an open whiskey bottle and an empty glass on the table in front of him, Logan stared across the room.

Daryl stood still, uncertain whether he should remain or leave, and in either event whether he should close the door behind him, when Logan looked up at him. "Thank you for this opportunity, Mister Bates," said Daryl.

"You're the Ingram boy," said Logan, reminding himself. His hand motioned Daryl, the only other person in the room, to a dark leather buttoned cushioned sofa facing his. "Sit down. Call me

Logan, your parents do."

Daryl sat in that second sofa. Logan pulled himself upright in his.

"What made you want to be an intern here, of all places?" asked Logan. "I'm glad you're here, but why here?"

"Doesn't everybody want to be a Congressional intern?"

"Only people who haven't been a Congressional intern want to be one."

Daryl laughed, before realizing he probably shouldn't have. "I want to help you implement your policies," said Daryl, like he was making another speech at school or college. "My family and I believe in you and the values for which you stand."

This time, Logan laughed. "Your parents are good people, good friends to my wife and me," he said, reaching towards his bottle of whiskey and glass. "You are older than twenty-one, aren't you?"

"I don't drink alcohol."

"You might want to start," said Logan, as he poured whiskey into his glass. "It can be your excuse to turn down worse substances you'll be offered."

"I was offered worse substances in college."

Logan sat back in his sofa, bringing his whiskey glass close to him. "In Washington," he said, "it's the good stuff: best quality, and expensive, including the whiskey."

Daryl looked again at the whiskey bottle. He didn't recognize the name on the label. Through the years Daryl had heard Logan speak in Florida, at his family home and elsewhere, he'd never before heard him talk of liquor. He'd never before sounded so self-absorbed.

"I should be fundraising now," admitted Logan. "As soon as one election's won, we start raising funds for the next. I get to spend time with your parents, which is nice, but I also spend time with people not so nice. They probably hold me in the same contempt that I hold them, but I've got votes and influence, they think, and they have money, so we're bedfellows. All most of us seem to do in this place is raise money for re-election. Most of the work we do is whatever those donors expect us to do."

Almost two years to the next elections for the House of Representatives had seemed so long a time that Daryl hadn't considered them, but they suddenly seemed so soon. "You have policies," said Daryl. "My family agrees with your demands that

America do more to redress Climate Change. The planet is dying and we're killing it."

Logan laughed, again. "Do you know why we talk so much about climate?" he asked.

"The scientific evidence is conclusive."

"Have you studied the scientific evidence?" asked Logan. "I haven't, and even if I tried, I wouldn't understand it. We trust what we're told because it suits us. It suits people who think we have nothing else to fear, nothing else to trust, because we want desperately to fear and desperately to trust. We want to think we're doing something good about the planet in a hundred years' time because we're ruining this country now. We want people fretting for a future long after they're dead, so they're not paying attention to the present."

Daryl stared at him, looking for reasons to be there. "Aren't Democrats supposed to help poor people?" he asked.

Again, Logan laughed, albeit more briefly this time. "Do we think we'd have taken up Republican support for immigration if we still protected poor people?" he asked. "We help rich people thinking they're helping poor people they hope they never meet."

Daryl shook his head. "Don't we support increasing the minimum wage and affordable health care?"

"We do when our donors don't mind," said Logan, "and I know your parents support them, but other donors object. The best thing is when I oppose them but other Congressmen pass them, or I support them but other Congressmen stop them, then everyone's happy. Keeping our Congressional seats means leaving our overlords in place, doing what they demand, so we can do something of what they let us do. That's the reason we first came here and reason we keep coming back. The trouble is: I'm having trouble remembering what I wanted to do and anything I've done."

Daryl gave Logan time to remember. Time didn't seem to help. "Have we become like Republicans?" asked Daryl.

"Republicans hate poor people," said Logan. "Democrats don't think about them. Even the immigrants thinking about their race aren't thinking about the poor among them, although they'll help their poor before they deliberately help any other poor. I'm learning to respect them for it, now that I've stopped pretending they don't."

Daryl sat silently, with nothing more to say and leaving Logan time to drink. If Logan were intoxicated then Daryl could dismiss everything he said, but he wasn't. Besides, Daryl's uncle once advised him that people were more likely to be truthful when intoxicated than sober. If Logan was sober, then perhaps he was joking.

"I'm sorry if I'm shattering your illusions," Logan apologized, "but you might as well hear it from me as you will from staffers and other interns. You'll hear a lot from a lot of people in a lot of under-stuffed bars and overstuffed parties, but not believing everything you hear doesn't mean you should disbelieve it all."

Daryl looked around Logan's private office, with more time to dwell upon it than he'd had when first he entered the open door. Among the photographs on his wall was one of Logan in Daryl's family home, with Daryl's parents and several donors from his district at one of their events.

Logan interrupted his recollections. "If you're wondering whether to tell your parents about this this, then don't," said Logan. "I'll be telling them the next time I speak with them, the next time they call with plans to host more fundraising. Your parents don't need me. Your parents bought you this internship and good for you and me they did; you can afford to be unpaid because your parents can afford you to be unpaid. Since this election I've realized will be my last, I've thought more and more of my predicament."

"Why would you retire?"

Logan held up his glass to see the whiskey in it, without drinking any. "The pundits are saying this will be my final term," he explained. "They say that what they call changing demographics in our district will mean I'll lose the Democratic nomination next time. Do you know what people mean by changing demographics, Daryl?"

"People aging?"

Logan laughed; Daryl had often seen Logan laugh, but never quite as frequently as he laughed that morning. "You would think that," said Logan. "Age is all they teach you, isn't it? Age, and gender, but age and gender have nothing to do with it. We talk about age and gender denigrating our opponents and supporting ours until we can't talk anymore, but it's not age and gender. I love Latinos and Hispanics, I never understood the difference, but why do you think I've kept talking about them?"

Daryl shook his head. "Latinos are from all of Latin American," he answered. "Hispanics are Spanish speakers; we studied Spanish at school."

Logan continued threatening to drink his next sip of whiskey from the glass near his mouth, without quite doing so. "Demographic is another of those words we use when we mean race," he explained. "I've supported immigration, documented and not, because supporting it seemed proper, and when we thought we were getting votes with all these immigrants, even after Republicans weren't getting their votes after admitting them and giving them amnesties, but we weren't really getting votes any more than Republicans did. We were getting the Democratic Party votes, while losing the Democratic Party."

Daryl nodded, remembering conversations with his parents. "We appreciated immigrants, all immigrants, for their support," he said. "They're good people."

"I used to presume they'd be more grateful to us," lamented Logan, "and they are grateful to us when we're competing with white candidates who aren't as welcoming of them as I've been, but they drop us once one of their own is standing. I like Barack Obama, we all do, but he's convinced them that anyone can be elected into anything in America, so now they're standing and they're voting for their own. Immigrant candidates count on their race to support them. White candidates can't; that would be racist."

Daryl pulled back a little in his seat. It was not a time to speak.

"Latinos get Latino votes," continued Logan, "Arabs get Arab votes, and so on. White people treat them better than they treat each other, so they used to vote for us ahead of voting for each other, but now most of them figure they'll do better by ganging up against us. They're winning and can't help but win. Those Democratic voters are voting us away."

Daryl wanted a more congenial explanation. "Do they worry that you're not representing them?" he asked.

Again Logan laughed. "We're representing them more than representing you," he insisted, "but we can't be them."

"Why then do you keep calling for more immigrants?"

Logan took that next sip of whiskey, throwing it too quickly down his throat to have enjoyed it. "Now that we're starting to realize what we're losing," he said, "do you think we still want them here? In twenty-four months, those immigrants are going to fire me from the only job I know and I can't stop them, without risking what we have left."

"The Republicans promise to cut immigration."

"Some Republicans say they will," said Logan, "others hint they will, and we'll keep criticizing them for doing so, but they won't. Too many Americans want cheap labor for them to do anything, and Republicans keep thinking they can sell themselves electorally to people who aren't buying them or us. They'll lose their party as surely as we're losing ours, but they're Republicans so they won't care."

Logan spoke with a candor that Daryl had never before heard, except about matters tame and unimportant. "We'll always vote for you," said Daryl.

The Congressman smiled. "Thank you, son, but there's not enough of you and me to keep me here."

"Why not tell America what you've told me?"

Again Logan laughed, although his laughing was becoming meeker each time he did. "If I was jumping for joy for our fate," he sighed, "with America's changing demographics they'd call me progressive, but I'm not, so they'd call me a bigot. Meanwhile, our Hispanic challengers being confident those demographics will elect them will be praised for being in touch with their communities. Those demographics aren't changing in the countries from which people are coming here."

"If this is your last term," persisted Daryl, "what can you lose by speaking out?"

Logan shook his head. "Why don't all the other Congress members in their final terms, or after they've retired, say what I'm saying?" he asked. "We don't, because we want to keep our friendships and relationships. I'm hoping to have more time with your parents, where we can raise funds for something more important than my successor's electoral chest. We want to be ambassadors or envoys, nominees to government and judicial bodies, or just members of the best golf and country clubs. If we learn nothing else in Congress, we learn to play golf."

Daryl also sighed, wondering how long he would remain there. Washington outside was very cold. Washington inside was worse.

Logan spoke again. "This is politics, son..."

"I'm not your son."

"You can dream all you like, but if you want to change the game then you've got to be part of the game. Otherwise, you'll be another short-termer who goes back home to the backwoods complaining about those pompous clowns in Washington to people who already agreed with you, slowly realizing how inconsequential you are."

"You're not a short-termer, Logan," Daryl corrected him. "You're in your seventh term, and you're going home in two years' time with those two years knowing you're inconsequential."

His hand holding that whiskey glass, Logan studied Daryl. "I am inconsequential, aren't I?" said Logan. "Interns are meant to learn, but here you are teaching me."

"There must be something you can do," pleaded Daryl, "something you can try to do?"

"The Supreme Court keeps us from saving America, or doing anything worthwhile. It confines us to little things that hardly really matter."

"Start with what you want to do," suggested Daryl, becoming quite the mentor to the man still something of a mentor to him, "then see what we can do."

Logan reached forward and laid his glass, with a little whiskey left in it, on the table. He stood up, removed his jacket, and slung it over his sofa. He ran his fingers around his waist, forcing his shirt back into his trousers, and began to walk around his private office. "If I were sitting at my home in Florida in two or more years' time," he said, without facing Daryl, "looking back on this time in Washington, looking back on this morning with you now, what would I wish I'd done, or tried to do?"

Still seated at his sofa, reluctant to disturb him, Daryl watched him walk. He listened to him talk, not certain Logan was addressing him. Logan would answer the question he'd set himself, without Daryl thinking he could contribute.

"Voters know they're being lied to," mused Logan, "but don't know who the liars are and can't particularize the lies. Telling everyone the truths that I've told you and more that I've not told you would be a start. Telling everybody else to tell the truth would follow, although I don't think they'll oblige. One or two might, knowing they're in their final terms, so I should try to encourage them all to get out of their holes, or offices."

Logan walked behind his big dark timber desk. He continued around and in front of it again.

"We need to let people tell the truth," continued Logan, "not just people we agree with. The only way people might believe us is if they know we've given other points of view the same chances to be heard. If we're confident we're right and because we can't be certain that we are, then we need to let people contradict us, while we keep telling the truth ourselves. We can't silence them because we think they're fools and liars, because they might think the same of us. One or both of us might be right."

Logan stopped at a shelf. He picked up and held, without obviously admiring, a crystal eagle, with a golden beak and claws.

"We need to reduce our need to raise money," said Logan, returning the eagle to the shelf. "Banning gifts and payments to Congressmen, political parties, and campaigns won't stop donors funding us by other means." He resumed walking around his private office. "I don't want to stop campaigns based upon issues, but we could ban all political advertising for the month before elections. Instead, television and other networks must provide five minutes time, a week before the election, to each of the candidates. Internet providers can't block political content at any time; candidates can make our pitches there, for voters to see and hear or not."

"That's good," said Daryl, "but it won't solve our demographic problem."

"There's a lot of truth to say about our demographic problem, much more than my small story."

"Your small story is also mine."

Logan stopped in front of Daryl, looking down but not really down at him. "This country wasn't born with universal suffrage," said Logan. "What country was, keeping everybody happy? What if I told you that universal suffrage has failed, that universal suffrage is unfair? What if I said the people who built this country, like your family, deserved votes that other people don't? We'd allocate other races seats in Congress so they could elect their own, but their seats should be fewer than ours."

Daryl sat up higher in his sofa. He'd already been sitting high.

"We'd treat them all more equally than they treat each other," continued Logan, "we've already seen some of what they think of each other, when they don't need each other's votes. They're better at representing their own than they are at representing each other, and they're not even trying to represent us. I'm not sure even your parents, smart as they are, can see how little other races represent us, when they realize they don't need to."

Daryl shook his head. "I'm sorry," he said, "I can't believe that."

Logan smiled. "Listen to this," he said, walking to his desk. He reached his hand down to press a button.

The sound of a ringing telephone came through a speaker there, before the click of it being answered. "Renata Sanchez," answered a distant voice.

"Renata, Logan Bates, I've got a man with problems here who thought he was in my district but he's in yours, Daryl Ingram. Can you see him?"

"You deal with him, will you Logan?"

"He is Hispanic, Renata, I thought you could help."

"Send him over then."

"Wait," said Logan, looking at Daryl while he paused. "Not to worry, Renata, looks like I can help him."

She hung up. Logan pressed a button. The speaker stopped sounding. "She'll have forgotten your name by the time she meets you," Logan told Daryl, "if she ever meets you."

"That's one person."

Logan began walking towards Daryl. "I can call any other immigrant Congressman," said Logan, "Democrat or Republican, change your race or religion to match, and get the same replies. Unless they know you carry enough votes and those votes matter, or enough money and money matters, busy people are too busy with their own to worry about you."

Silence ensued; Logan had proven his point. "Do you want seven pointless terms in Congress," asked Daryl, "or one fruitful term?"

Logan sat back onto his sofa, facing Daryl, more upright than he'd previously sat that morning. "Packs of journalists skulk about this building," said Logan, before smiling. "Shall I feed them?"

Daryl smiled, with a dream as big as any he had known. "You could call a press conference in front of the Lincoln Memorial," he suggested.

"I could ask the House leadership to let me address the House Democratic Caucus," said Logan, unmoved by Daryl's dream, "but they won't be interested. I'd be better talking to Congress members in my position, Democrats and Republicans, to see if they're as relaxed about our demographic destiny as they claim to be, as I've claimed to be."

"Americans want to know you care as much about their future as you do about yours," Daryl reminded him.

Logan nodded. "If discrimination in our favor is right," he said, "then discrimination in their favor is right. God knows, we've pushed discrimination against them long enough."

The Congressman stood up again, collected his jacket from the sofa, and dressed back into it. He then bounced on out of that room.

He might have headed to the journalists. He might have headed to his colleagues. There'd been too much bounce in his step for Logan not to have headed somewhere.

Daryl remained alone in Logan's private office, seated in that sofa, collecting his breath. Outside, through the open office door, uproar would arise to hear Logan's call to change. Daryl would have a story to tell of his small role in so great a moment as was coming, wherever it led. There'd be more for his parents to do; they'd be thrilled to see Logan back to life. Daryl needed time to steady.

On the small table in front of him, between him and the empty sofa, lay more than just Logan's abandoned glass and whiskey bottle. Also lying there, less obvious than the whiskey, was a round pewter trinket box. From that box shone, with the light reflected from it, the seal of the United States Congress. The seal was never more impressive.

A Latina woman entered the office carrying a small bundle of newspapers, one of which she placed on the low table in front of Daryl, beside the bottle, glass, and trinket box. After seeing Daryl seated there, she glanced around the otherwise empty office, before looking back at Daryl. "Should you be here?" she asked him.

"I'm Logan Bates' new intern."

She rolled her eyes. She then departed.

No more noise came from outside the office door. Daryl stood up from the sofa and turned around, listening for any sound he could. All he heard were ordinary voices from Logan's outer office, much like those he'd heard all morning.

Perhaps Daryl should have followed him, although Logan would have told him to follow him if he should. Perhaps Daryl should return to that outer office, without getting in people's way.

Again, Daryl looked around the room. With those pictures on the walls and ornaments in sight, Logan's private office never seemed more like a slice of Florida, especially Daryl's home district, than it seemed then. The office was alive with Daryl's thoughts of Logan making change to Washington like he'd often said he would, but plainly hadn't.

Daryl would have walked around the room examining every picture and ornament, but that would be presumptive. It might also be rude, and anybody could appear at the open door to see him. Standing where he stood, beside the sofa where Logan had directed him, in the place that Logan left him, was defensible. Around him was enough for him to see, in which he could bask, in a Congressional private office.

Through the open office door, walking quickly, appeared a female staffer Daryl had already met, wearing a sleek blue dress perhaps for being a Democrat; he'd met all of Logan's staff that morning, he thought. Seeing Daryl, she stopped, stepped quickly towards him, and glanced at Logan's empty desk. She looked back at Daryl. "Lunch today at Cactus Cantina," she told him. "Tex-Mex, all of us, twelve thirty from here. Can't remember who's buying, I'll tell you on the way so you can pretend to thank him." She stepped back and through the door.

Daryl again stood alone. Logan might be away so long Daryl should return to the outer offices, waiting to be told what to do.

Logan reappeared at the door. The bounce in his step had gone as he trudged slowly towards Daryl, but not towards him, veering to the table where his whiskey bottle remained. Without filling his almost empty glass, Logan took it in his hand and slumped back into the sofa in which he sat when Daryl first entered that morning.

With Logan sitting, Daryl sat back down where Logan first invited him to sit. Standing while Logan sat would have been impolite.

"I'm not fruitful," confessed Logan, glass in hand. "I still want to keep my friendships and relationships. I want to be an ambassador or envoy, a nominee to some government or judicial body, and a member of a decent golf or country club. I've learnt to play a clever game of golf in Washington."

"What about your disappointments, looking back in two years' time on your Congressional career?"

Logan drank his whiskey, emptying the glass. "You be the

candidate," he told Daryl, "after you've developed a cogent political philosophy. The task I'm giving you, my intern, is to write what we have said and more into that philosophy, making as certain as you can that what you write is true, but don't worry that you can't ever be completely certain. Get everything clear in your head so you know where your head is, and where you want us to be. Get everything clear on paper so I can support you, or not, and other people can understand you, if they're willing to try."

Daryl shook his head. "Do people want philosophy?" he asked.

"Let them critique you," Logan advised him, comfortably Daryl's mentor again. "Listen to facts and reason, ready to improve your philosophy discarding anything you learn is wrong, but you stick to whatever you conclude is correct. We live in a time when facts about people and our most natural of feelings are berated for being bigotry, among white people."

Logan returned his empty glass to the table. Touching the whiskey bottle, he pointed his eyes to Daryl, with an inquiring nod.

Daryl shook his head. He might try a sip of whiskey back at his hotel bar that evening, where no one else could see.

Without pouring more whiskey, Logan sat back only as far as the front edge of his sofa, as if he were about to stand and work. "Maybe the philosophy we need is just cherishing truth and knowledge," suggested Logan. "Perhaps we need simply pragmatism: embracing whatever makes people safest, happiest, and most fulfilled. We might merely need again to respect human nature.

"She would have denied it, but all my Hispanic challenger offered her people was nationalism and it was almost enough to win. Next election, it will be. Don't let people convince you that nationalism is bad: we're suffering the alternative, while they hide nationalism of their own. The only nationalism, and only racism, they really oppose is ours."

10 AGED CARE

Her husband's federal government career had brought Margret Wilkie from Missouri to live in suburban Alexandria, Virginia. He died soon after he retired, before they'd decided whether to return to Missouri, move south, or remain where they were.

Remaining in Alexandria, with everything Margret knew and treasured, became easier than moving elsewhere. Their comfortable timber home had always felt cozy for feeling a little small, in spite of being two floors tall, so didn't feel too big after her husband died. More of Margret's friends remained nearby than had retired and gone to any other single place.

As Margret aged, her friends also aged. They visited her less often and she visited them less often. Eventually, they moved into nursing homes or other aged-care facilities, or passed away altogether.

Margret felt her body weaken, as her shoulders began to stoop. Her walk slowed to a shuffle. Her life and circumstance had left Margret childless, becoming lonely in her still comfortable nice home.

Instead of entering aged-care facilities, among other lonely people, agencies assisted elderly and sick people to stay in their private homes. For Margret, they offered her a little help to keep her home clean, to wash and iron her clothes, and even to drive her to the stores or occasionally a restaurant or anywhere else she wanted to go; she had little else on which to spend her money. They also offered someone to visit her.

The agency Margret contacted offered her Yahnaa, among the caregivers on its roll. From the vantage of Margret's age, Yahnaa was young, although Margret remembered when thirty-seven years of age wasn't young. Before coming to America with her husband and children, Yahnaa cared for her parents in Kathmandu, which Margret concluded meant she would be good at caring for other elderly people. She spoke English and Nepali, which sounded, to Margret, interesting. Yahnaa also had a driver's license.

Certain that anyone caring for old people in their homes must be nice, as indeed Margret was certain that everyone was nice, she accepted that offer. Initially, Yahnaa would come to Margret's home each Tuesday and Friday for three hours at a time, from ten o'clock in the morning until one o'clock in the afternoon, to help Margret in any way that Margret asked. Margret might later extend those visits.

The first Tuesday morning Yahnaa was due to come, Margret prepared for her arrival more like Yahnaa was a guest than a paid helper. In her long beige woolen skirt and wearing a slightly paler beige cardigan concealing her woolen blouse, Margret hung pearl earrings from her ears and draped her pearl necklace around her neck; she rarely had cause to wear them anymore.

Margret checked her lounge room that everything was neat. She puffed up the cushions on the sofa. She dusted her ornaments on the sideboard.

Hanging from the small lines in her laundry, Margret's washed clothes had dried. Ironing them would be the first task she asked of Yahnaa.

The time, ten o'clock, that Yahnaa was due to arrive neared; in Margret's home were several old clocks, from her years in life that time meant more than it normally still meant. Everything in Margret's home seemed in order, she assured herself, as she rested in an armchair in her lounge room.

The clock struck ten o'clock. No sound came from outside.

Margret waited. A minute or two later, she stepped across the room to the window from which she looked down her driveway and front path to the street. No person was there. No unfamiliar car was parked there.

She remained at the window, looking out and down for any movement of a car or person coming. The longer she remained there, the more she realized she had never before waited there for a visitor. Her friends, when they used to visit, could be a little early or a little late, as Margret could be a little early or a little late visiting them, but none of them ever minded. If Margret expected Yahnaa to be punctual because she was paying her, or paying the agency that paid her, then Margret was probably being unfair.

Margret left the window. She prepared herself a cup of tea, keeping the kitchen clean as she did, always listening for the sound of someone at the door. She sat with her cup of tea back in her armchair in the lounge room. The time approached ten thirty.

Another ten minutes elapsed before a knock came from the front door. Margret hurried to answer it, opening the door to a short woman she'd didn't recognize, wearing a bright red sash over a long bright red dress. From her pale brownish complexion, dark brown eyes, and long black rustic hair, Margret could believe she was Nepalese, without knowing what Nepalese looked like. In the woman's hand was a large dark bag, as a woman might take shopping, but already carrying something.

"You Mrs. Wilkie?" the woman asked through a thick accent, her eyes drifting to Margret's earrings.

"Yahnaa?" asked Margret, although it obviously was. "Please, come in."

Margret stepped back, as the woman stepped past her, into the hallway. There, she stopped to look up at the ceiling, with its hanging crystal lights, and look around the walls of old framed sketches.

"I was expecting you at ten," said Margret.

"I have errands." Yahnaa proceeded into the lounge room.

Margret followed her. "I've been looking forward to you helping me with the ironing," said Margret.

Her bag left standing on the floor against the wall, Yahnaa explored the lounge room, inspecting it as if it were a museum, except that visitors at museums didn't touch exhibits. From the sideboard, Yahnaa picked up Margret's colorful little wooden replica of Gadsby's Tavern, only three quarters of an inch thick, examining it. "This expensive?" asked Yahnaa.

"I bought that with my late husband," Margret explained, not remembering the cost of anything she'd bought; she disliked discussing money. The value of her ornaments was sentimental, as was the value of most of what she owned and all of what she treasured. "I'm afraid the Unique jewelry store on King Street closed a long time ago, but the Tavern Museum is a lovely place to visit. We might be able to go there, one Tuesday or Friday?"

"American history not interest me," answered Yahnaa, as she returned the tavern replica to the sideboard.

She left it lying there, face down. Margret always kept it standing upright against the rear border of the sideboard, making it easy to see.

Yahnaa picked up the bluish ceramic vase beside it, holding it with one hand while she lifted off the lid, with its small ceramic bird that first attracted Margret to it. "This expensive?" asked Yahnaa.

"We bought that from the old Torpedo Factory," said Margret, "although we knew it only as an art center, not long before my husband died. It's a Phyllis Roderer, as a matter of fact."

Yahnaa returned the vase to the sideboard, a short way from where she'd picked it up. She left the lid and bird lying next to it.

She walked along, leaving Margret behind. Margret stood her replica tavern and vase on the sideboard where she liked them, with the bird lid back atop the vase.

Yahnaa walked past Margret's books, her reading glasses lying in front of them, without stopping, but she stopped at the small table by Margret's armchair. There stood Margret's empty teacup on a saucer. "Where I find tea?" asked Yahnaa.

Margret led Yahnaa to the kitchen, where she introduced her to the kettle and refrigerator, although they couldn't have been more obvious. Margret opened the high cupboard, for Yahnaa to see the shelf on which Margret kept her boxes of teabags.

Yahnaa reached her arm across Margret and up to the shelf, took a box, and brought it close to her. "This only tea you have?" she asked, examining the box.

"I'm afraid so."

Yahnaa sighed. "Have to do," she said, resting the box of teabags on the counter near the kettle. She checked the kettle carried plenty of water, and set it boiling.

Margret watched her. "When might we get to the ironing, Yahnaa?" she asked.

"You start."

"I was rather hoping you might iron."

Yahnaa looked around at the closed cupboard doors above her and those beneath the counter. She opened the full-length pantry cupboard. "Where cups?" she asked.

Margret stepped towards one high cupboard and opened the door to the crockery. She brought down two cups and saucers she rested on the counter.

Yahnaa placed a teabag in the cup nearest her. The kettle boiled, and she poured the hot water into her cup.

"May I also have a cup of tea?" asked Margret.

Yahnaa picked up her cup and saucer. "I finish now," she said, walking away and out of the kitchen.

Margret prepared herself a cup of tea, before following where she thought Yahnaa had gone. She found Yahnaa in the lounge room, resting in Margret's first choice of armchair, drinking her tea. Margret took another armchair. "I would like us to get to the ironing," said Margret.

"You live in nice street," said Yahnaa, her cup in her hand.

"Do you live nearby?" asked Margret. The information the agency had given her about Yahnaa did not include her home address or telephone number; all contact between clients and caregivers was to be through the agency, except during the caregivers' visits.

"Too expensive."

"Your English is very good," said Margret.

"I study in Nepal, only thing worth studying English, so I come to America."

Margret smiled. "You seem to have settled in very well," she said.

Yahnaa looked into her cup. "I get used to your tea," she said.

Margret continued drinking from her cup. Her lounge room was slightly different from her perspective in that armchair, as against her usual one.

"You have cake?" asked Yahnaa.

"I'm afraid I don't normally eat cake."

"I see what you got." Carrying her cup, but her saucer left behind, Yahnaa stood up and left the lounge room.

Her cup and saucer in hand, Margret followed Yahnaa back to the kitchen. She found Yahnaa standing at the open refrigerator door, her cup standing behind her on the counter.

Yahnaa removed from the refrigerator a small plastic container, unfastened the lid, and opened it. There she saw several slices of cold roast beef. "How old meat?" she asked.

"I bought it yesterday," said Margret, resting her cup and saucer on the counter.

Yahnaa held the open container near her nose. "Smell okay," she said.

Margret closed the refrigerator door. "That was to be my lunch, Yahnaa," she said.

With her fingertips, Yahnaa tentatively picked up the uppermost slice of beef; Margret wondered what she feared from it. Yahnaa bit it, slowly chewing it.

While Yahnaa ate, Margret went to a cupboard, opened it, and removed from it a plate. She laid the plate on the counter beside the container of roast beef. Margret went to the cutlery drawer, opened it, and pulled from it a knife and fork, with which she set the remaining roast beef from the container on the plate. When she finished, Margret laid the knife and fork on the counter beside the plate, and stepped back, out of Yahnaa's way.

Yahnaa took the plate of cold roast beef in her hand, leaving the knife and fork behind as she carried the plate from the room. Margret followed her back to the lounge room, where Yahnaa sat back in the armchair in which she'd previously sat: Margret's armchair. Holding the plate near her face, probably more for her convenience than from fear of spilling anything, Yahnaa again used her fingers to pick up the uppermost slice of cold beef. She ate it.

"I'm sorry," Margret apologized, still standing. "Don't people use knives and forks in Nepal?"

Yahnaa continued eating. "This good," she said.

"Can I get you more tea?" asked Margret.

"You know how I drink it."

Margret returned to the kitchen, where she prepared two cups of tea; her unfinished cup had cooled and she emptied it in the sink. Waiting for the kettle to boil, Margret returned the knife and fork to the cutlery drawer. She placed the empty plastic container in the dishwasher.

Soon, carrying a tray with two cups of tea on saucers and a plate of cookies, Margret returned to the lounge room. From the tray that Margret held in front of her, after resting her plate of cold beef on her lap, Yahnaa removed the plate of cookies, as well as the cup nearest to her, leaving the saucer behind.

Margret rested the tray with Yahnaa's saucer on a small table. She took the second saucer and cup, and returned to her new armchair.

Yahnaa looked around, before resting her plate of cookies on the small table beside the chair: the table on which Margret rested plates and saucers when she sat in that armchair. Yahnaa sipped from her tea. She ate more cold beef from the plate on her lap.

Margret spoke up. "When do you think you could help me with the ironing, Yahnaa?" she asked.

"I iron for my husband and children."

"I would like some help," said Margret. "I know how much help you were to your parents, in Kathmandu."

"They my parents, they not as old as you but my country, children respect parents. We look after parents."

"My husband and I were always too busy for children," explained Margret. "That's why I'm so glad you've come to America. I appreciate all your help."

"You not my mother," said Yahnaa, eating the beef that would have been Margret's lunch, between sips of tea Margret had prepared, sitting in the armchair normally Margret's in which to sit. "I here because you pay me, but you not expect me help you because I help my mother."

Margret sat with only her tea, in her unfamiliar armchair. "The agency suggested you would help me iron?" she said.

"You think I do everything you say because you pay me?"

"Not everything…"

"I not your slave."

Margret thought it better not to say anything. She thought of leaving her armchair to get a cookie from the plate on the table beside Yahnaa, but it had come to seem too far away to step.

When she'd finished eating the beef, Yahnaa put that empty plate on the small table beside her. She then brought the plate of cookies from the table to her lap. She bit one cookie, chewed the portion in her mouth, and swallowed it. "You cook these?" she asked.

"Yesterday," answered Margret. "I baked them to share with you."

Yahnaa continued eating the cookies, between sips of tea. Sometimes, she looked around the room. Other times, she simply stared.

Margret watched her. Few people still visited for her to watch.

When Yahnaa finished eating the cookies, she returned that plate to the small table. She placed her cup beside it.

Margret stood up from her armchair, collected Yahnaa's empty plates, cup, and saucer on her tray, and carried the tray to the kitchen. She then returned to the lounge room, where Yahnaa lay reclined in her armchair.

"Please, Yahnaa," said Margret, "please could you at least stand with me while I iron?"

Yahnaa stood up, conspicuously stretching her muscles.

Leaving the lounge room, she explored each room downstairs she had not already seen: the dining room, the lesser lounge room. With Margret following her, she proceeded towards the rear of the house.

Margret became excited. "The laundry is through the door to your left," she said, hurrying closer to her.

Yahnaa passed that door; it was the first door she passed without opening. Margret reached it and stopped there, her hand on the handle.

"Please, Yahnaa," said Margret, "please?"

Yahnaa reached the door to the small rear lawn, which she opened. Stepping outside, she stopped, looking around at the trees and shrubs. "You look after this?" she asked.

Margret stood beside her. "A gardener comes every second week," said Margret, sighing with every point of conversation between them other than her ironing. Her husband had paid their gardener to keep the grounds before he died and Margret continued paying him to keep them afterwards, arranging for him to come days when he carried her garbage can to the sidewalk; Margret's thoughts were always more devoted to the interior of their home. "He's very helpful."

Yahnaa turned to face her. "You criticizing me?" she asked. "You saying I not helpful?"

"No."

Yahnaa turned away from her again. She again gazed around at the trees and shrubs that shielded the lawn from the upstairs windows of adjoining homes and shielded those upstairs windows from any person on the lawn.

What remained was very peaceful: a place that Margret sometimes sat, on the old bench close to the house, but to which she rarely brought even her rare visitors to her home. "If I brought my ironing and the ironing board outside," said Margret, "could I do the ironing while you sit here and we talk?"

Yahnaa began walking across the grass, until she stopped and turned around, looking up at the rear of the house. "Your home nicer than mine," she said.

"My husband and I worked very hard to buy it."

"My husband and I work hard," answered Yahnaa, still looking at the house, "but working for you not pay."

"I am paying you good money to assist me today."

Yahnaa looked back at Margret. "You paying agency," Yahnaa reminded her, "and agency pay me half money you pay it. You save a quarter money you pay by telling agency you canceling my visits, then paying three quarters to me."

Margret would save money and Yahnaa would earn more money, but the aged-care agency would lose its revenue. "Isn't that dishonest?" asked Margret, knowing that it was.

Yahnaa smiled. "You not tell them," she said. "I tell agency I not available times I come here. They not know I here. They think I home with my children; they not know my husband there. I do for other clients."

Margret continued staring at her, trying to understand her, although Margret's response to Yahnaa's proposal was always certain, to Margret. "I could never do that," said Margret. "I could never lie."

"You still have more money than I have. You still rich."

Margret remained still, before shaking her head. "I am sorry," she smiled.

Yahnaa walked back across the grass towards the house. She returned inside, leaving the rear door open behind her.

Margret followed her, closing the door behind them. Again she passed the closed laundry door, following Yahnaa along the hallway to the stairs. Yahnaa started to climb them.

"Yahnaa," called out Margret, "there is only my bedroom up there, along with rooms I don't use."

She continued climbing the stairs; Yahnaa might have been the first person other than Margret to climb them since Margret's husband died, so many years earlier. Margret followed Yahnaa up to the landing.

The bathroom door stood open, as it always did when the bathroom was unoccupied. Yahnaa could see as well as Margret that it was only a bathroom.

The first room Yahnaa entered was a study, with a handful of bank statements and the like on a desk and a small filing cabinet nearby. From the door, Margret watched Yahnaa stand near the desk, without touching any papers. "This your husband's?" asked Yahnaa.

"This study has always been mine," answered Margret, "since we came here." Not even her late husband entered it, so far as Margret could recall.

When Yahnaa finished there, Margret stepped back from the doorway to let her leave the room. Yahnaa proceeded along the landing to the next room: Margret's late husband's study, much like hers. Rarely had Margret entered it when her husband was alive. After he died, she'd checked his desk and filing cabinet for the papers she needed and removed them, leaving everything else behind. She had rarely again entered his study, remaining much as it was when he died, except occasionally to wipe away dust.

Yahnaa walked around Margret's late husband's study. Presumably for being so much like Margret's study, Yahnaa soon walked from it.

In the next room, where it had always been, stood Margret's dressing table and wardrobe. Margret watched Yahnaa open the wardrobe door, Yahnaa's eyes rolling across Margret's array of woolen skirts, cardigans, and blouses. With them were the finer dresses Margret stopped wearing after her husband died and after she stopped attending the dinners and other events for which she'd bought them. "Nice," said Yahnaa, before glancing down at the red dress and sash she wore. She then glanced across at the skirt, cardigan, and blouse that Margret wore, much like any in the wardrobe. "Too many," she said.

Margret noticed lying on her dressing table her jewelry box, from which she'd taken her pearl necklace and earrings that morning. Rather than hear Yahnaa tell her she had too much jewelry, Margret stepped behind Yahnaa to the dressing table. Margret picked up her jewelry box and turned back to Yahnaa, holding her jewelry box behind her.

Leaving the wardrobe door open, Yahnaa proceeded to Margret's dressing table. Margret stepped behind her, slipped her jewelry box in her wardrobe out of sight, and closed her wardrobe door.

From Margret's dressing table, Yahnaa picked up several bottles of potions and lotions, apparently reading the labels. She picked up several packets and small bottles of pills and tablets, apparently reading the labels. "You sick?" asked Yahnaa, opening a drawer of the dressing table to inspect its contents.

Margret couldn't immediately recall the contents of that drawer. "I'm old," she said.

"My parents old, without tricks; they had my sisters and me."

"I have you, too, Yahnaa," said Margret, "Tuesdays and Fridays, from ten until one, or longer."

Margret followed Yahnaa from her dressing room to the last room on the floor: Margret's bedroom, still with the queen-sized bed she'd shared with her late husband. Thankfully, Margret still dressed it neatly every day, with a quilt smoothly lain above the blankets, sheets, and pillows.

Against one wall remained Margret's late husband's wardrobe, still with his suits and other clothes. She should, in time, donate them to charity. There was a lot she should donate to charity.

Below the main window, overlooking the street, was a single chair, in which Margret sometimes liked to sit. It would also be useful for days when she needed a doctor or nurse to come.

Margret watched Yahnaa stand at the slightly better lit window side of her bed, where Margret normally slept. Yahnaa pressed her hand against the edge of the mattress, letting it spring back. "Nice," she said.

Bending forward, Yahnaa lifted the side of the quilt, dragging it over the bed. She exposed Margret's neatly folded cream-colored blankets, white sheets tucked into the mattress, and fluffy white pillows and pillowcases. Yahnaa pulled out the blankets and sheets, before slipping her shoes from her feet; Margret was grateful for that. In her bright red dress and with a bright red sash dragging from her, Yahnaa then climbed into the bed, lying face up. She rested her head against the pillow, and closed her eyes.

Margret shuffled to the side of the bed away from Yahnaa, which remained covered by the quilt. That was the side of the bed on which her late husband used to sleep, but Margret simply sat there, on the quilt, looking away from Yahnaa to the wall. Margret couldn't hear whether Yahnaa, behind her, was awake or asleep.

"Yahnaa," asked Margret, without looking at her, "are you like this with all your clients?"

"Why?"

"Are all your clients satisfied?"

"I Caregiver of the Month three times, getting gifts, and certificates."

Margret turned around to see Yahnaa still lying face up in Margret's bed, her head almost lost in the pillow, her eyes still closed. "We're supposed to report our opinions of caregivers," said Margret.

"One woman complain about me," said Yahnaa, her eyes

remaining closed. "I tell agency she racist. They not send her another caregiver."

Margret sat watching her, choosing her words more carefully than she usually needed to choose them. "Do you tell all your clients about her?" asked Margret.

Her eyes still closed, Yahnaa smiled. "Only clients needing warning," she said.

Margret stood up and stepped away from the mattress. She stepped around her bed towards the main window, where she slipped into her solitary chair. "So," said Margret, supposedly to herself but for Yahnaa to hear, "a client who doesn't want a Nepalese caregiver, needs to find another reason not to choose her, not to accept her."

Yahnaa's eyes opened. She slowly sat up in Margret's bed.

"A client who wants an American caregiver," continued Margret, "needs to think of a reason for that caregiver that nobody knows has anything to do with her race, such as being able to talk about American history, or come to American museums, or cook apple pie, hash browns, or chocolate chip cookies."

Yahnaa climbed up from the bed and stepped towards Margret in her chair. There, she stopped, standing close to Margret, looking down at Margret as Margret looked up at her. "I your caregiver, Mrs. Wilkie," said Yahnaa, "Margret." She inched a little closer to Margret. "You not be racist by complaining to agency about me."

Margret nodded. "I know I am being unfair," she said, "and I will apologize to the agency for being an imposition on so wonderful a caregiver as you, but I need you to make me Eggs Benedict."

"What Eggs Benedict?"

"Don't you know?"

"I learn."

"I am so sorry, Yahnaa," said Margret, "but I need Eggs Benedict cooked now."

"I tell agency I learn."

"I also need a Philadelphia cream cheesecake."

"You hire cook."

"Yes," said Margret, "I will telephone the agency now to say I am so sorry, but I should have hired a cook, and cancel your appointments here."

Yahnaa continued staring down at her. "Then you alone, Mrs.

Wilkie."

"I will be alone, unless I realize tomorrow that I can cook, and do need the assistance only of a caregiver."

"Then, I come Friday."

"I wish you could come on Friday," said Margret, "but I'll tell the agency that I am so embarrassed after the difficulty I have put you through today, that I couldn't possibly face you again. I feel so awful, I couldn't face another lovely Nepalese caregiver again. I might, sadly, have to see only American caregivers for a while, until I stop feeling as awful as I do about being so difficult for you today."

"You only want white people?"

"Will only white people help me?" asked Margret. "Should I be willing to take a chance that other races might, after my experience today?"

Yahnaa remained still, before slowly her attention left Margret. Looking around Margret's bedroom, Yahnaa soon faced the clock on the table beside Margret's bed. The time was not yet noon. "Do I still get paid for three hours, today?" she asked.

"You were forty minutes late."

Yahnaa faced Margret again, looking down at her. "You want me to tell agency you racist?"

Staring back up at Yahnaa, Margret took the time she needed before replying. "What would happen," asked Margret, "if I told the agency that you'd offered to shut them out of our arrangement: to come here and be paid directly by me, at a twenty-five percent discount, if I told the agency I was cancelling your service?"

"I tell agency not believe you because you racist. You lie because you hate Nepalese, because you want white people."

"What would happen if," resumed Margret, "when I was telling the agency about your offer, I said that you said other clients had done the same, and that the agency should check its records for your past clients who had cancelled their services, telephone those clients, and ask them whether they had continued with visits from you, paying you directly?"

"Why clients answer agency questions?"

"The agency would say it is investigating the matter as a health and safety issue," replied Margret. "Health and safety is particularly important to the elderly, and the agency can say, truthfully, that it needs to know who its caregivers see so it can maintain the necessary training. I expect the agency won't want to send you to any more clients knowing you would try to exclude it from its income, don't you?"

Yahnaa continued looking at Margret, before slowly turning and again looking around the room, up at the ceiling. "You rich," she told Margret, without looking at her, "you have all this money, and you try to keep my little money for you."

"No," Margret corrected her, "I'm only trying to keep it from you."

Again Yahnaa turned back to Margret. Her stance, looking down at Margret, probably meant more to Yahnaa than it meant to Margret.

"I'll tell the agency," explained Margret, "that I'll pay its money for the three-hour service today, but that you want the money due to you donated to charity: I know, Gadsby's Tavern Museum. You do want that, don't you Yahnaa, rather than me telling the agency that you invite clients to exclude it from being paid? I can check with the Museum that it received your donation from the agency."

Yahnaa continued staring at her, before slowly turning away. She walked from the room.

Margret rose from her chair and followed Yahnaa back to the stairs. She followed her stepping slowly back down.

She followed Yahnaa back to the lounge room, where Yahnaa retrieved her bag from the floor by the wall. Margret still didn't know what was in it.

Margret followed her back to the hallway and front door, which Yahnaa opened. Before departing, she turned back to Margret. "I not like your house," she told Margret. "I not like your tea, or food, or bed. I not like you."

Yahnaa turned around and left, leaving the door open behind her. Margret closed and locked the door.

Margret leant her back against her closed door to her solitary home, breathing long but easily again. At the far end of her home remained her laundry, in which her dried clothes still awaited being ironed.

She knew she should tell the agency the truth about Yahnaa, in order to save other clients and the agency from her, although Margret expected there to be many more like Yahnaa behaving like her; they had no reason not to. Margret would not tell the agency she only wanted American caregivers to come; that would be truth the agency would not accept, however many more caregivers like Yahnaa it employed.

Enough of her energy restored, Margret drifted back to her lounge room, where she slumped back into her favorite armchair. She removed her pearl earrings from her ears and pearl necklace from her neck; she'd soon return them to her jewelry box upstairs and return her jewelry box from her wardrobe to her dressing table.

From her armchair, the lounge room was again as she recalled. Margret was again as she recalled. Everything seemed again as it had been early that morning, before Yahnaa came, until Margret's roving eyes caught her sideboard. Her colorful little replica of Gadsby's Tavern and her bluish vase with the small bird on the lid had gone.

11 NEIGHBORS

Among most races on earth, people keep their aged parents. They raise children expecting those children to keep them when they age.

By two decades into the twenty-first century, white people no longer did. They expected immigrants to keep their aged parents, for a fee, of course. (White people expected to be able to buy almost anything.) Without children of their own, they expected immigrants to keep them when their time for care came.

Money can buy many things from people willing to sell, but not everyone is willing to sell. Even people willing to sell don't sell everything.

Her money bought elderly Margret Wilkie an hour or so in her suburban home in Alexandria, Virginia with a Nepalese woman Yahnaa, supposedly a caregiver. It didn't buy Yahnaa's care. Nor did it buy her honesty, if indeed Yahnaa had honesty to sell.

After that bad experience, Margret's visits from an American caregiver were better. The two of them chatted while the caregiver ironed Margret's clothes and performed other chores, even if she lacked the devotion of Margret's niece, her closest relative.

Aside from that niece, who lived in upstate New York with her husband and children so could only visit Margret every few months, and now her American caregiver each Tuesday and Friday, few people still visited Margret's home. So the Saturday morning Margret heard a knock on her front door, she was really quite excited; her niece always telephoned beforehand to arrange her visits, so it wouldn't be her.

Margret was sitting in her favorite cushioned armchair in her lounge room, dressed in another of her long cream woolen skirts and wearing another of her slightly paler cream cardigans concealing her woolen blouse, as she wore every day. She rested her cup of tea on the saucer on the small table beside her, imagining what old friend or friends she'd not seen for so long might have knocked on her door. It might be a former colleague of her late husband, who'd worked so long for the federal government in Washington.

She stood up from her chair. The visitors might be her former neighbors who'd returned home to Arkansas after that husband's retirement from his federal government career, and who'd promised to visit Margret again someday.

Margret hurried from her lounge room into her hallway, as much as she could hurry at her age. The visitors might be her other former neighbors who'd retired home to Oklahoma, although they'd insisted Margret visit them because they never wanted to be back near Washington again. Margret really didn't want to travel so far from home, anymore.

She reached the front door, unlocked it, and opened it, to none of those people. Instead, five rough young men crowded the space outside her door. They wore an array of shirts and skivvies emblazoned with corporate, sporting, and university names worn many times over, along with denim jeans faded to varying degrees. With their pale brownish complexions, dark brown eyes, and black hair, Margret's experience of Yahnaa two weeks earlier suggested they might be Nepalese.

Margret continued holding the door. It was a thick heavy timber door, painted white when it had been meant to be inviting. That moment, Margret didn't intend it to be inviting.

"Are you Margret Wilkie?" one of the young men asked her, in a manner gruff to say the least. Taller and heavier built than the other men, and decidedly taller and heavier built than Margret, he stood at the front of the group closest to Margret, glaring down at her. Unlike Yahnaa, he spoke without a foreign accent, although his American accent was much coarser than the voices with which Margret was familiar.

That the question was asked in such a manner, and that five young men were there for one young man to ask it, left Margret reticent to answer. "May I please inquire who you are?" she asked the man who'd asked her the question, although she really asked all of them.

The only man to speak spoke again. "Are you Margret Wilkie?" he persisted.

Margret continued looking up at him. "Why would you like to know?" she asked.

"Margret Wilkie is a liar. She lied about a woman failing to give her any care. She lied about that woman trying to cheat money from her employer. She lied about the woman stealing from her house."

Margret stepped back, pushing the door closed, but one of the young men stepped forward. His body kept the door open, his leg and foot stretched forward obstructing the door.

Keeping her hand on the door, although unable to close it any further and unable to resist if that young man pushed it further open, Margret reached around the door to face them again. That same young man who'd done all the talking was holding her door open. "Are you Yahnaa's family?" asked Margret.

That young man obstructing the door didn't answer. A man behind him did. "I know her brother," he said.

That first young man spoke again. "I've talked to Yahnaa," he told Margret. "She has a family to feed but lost her job because of your lies. Aren't you ashamed?"

"I told the truth."

"No!" the man snapped. He began pushing open the door.

Margret's meagre muscles, such as they were, taut and tightening, were too weak to resist him. She slowly stepped back, retreating from her door she could not defend into her hallway, as that first man stepped into her home. Behind him, the other men stepped.

Slowly, stepping carefully, facing the young men stepping towards her, Margret retreated along her short hallway. Glancing back and down just enough to keep her footing on the rugs and floorboards, she retreated into her lounge room.

The young men continued stepping in unison with her, their eyes set upon her. Margret thought of reaching for the telephone to call the police, but the young men would stop her before she could. Unable to fight, unable to flee, she slipped into the last place she might feel almost comfortable: her cushioned armchair.

Her home no longer the haven it felt only a short time earlier, and had felt throughout her decades living there, that leading young man stopped in front of her. The other young men gathered around, standing in a spreading semicircle confronting her, glaring down at little Margret in her chair.

That leading young man stepped across the floor to the small table beside Margret's armchair. He picked up her cup of tea, looked inside it, and seemed to smell it or check its temperature; it was probably cold, thought Margret. He returned the cup to the saucer. "You lied," he told Margret, stepping back to his space at the head of the semicircle, again standing in front of her, glaring down at her. "You now have to call Yahnaa's employer and say you lied, saying you insist she get her job back and wanting to hire her again."

"I can't," Margret pleaded with him. "Another caregiver now comes."

"Is she Nepalese?"

"She's American."

"You lied to give an American the job."

"I don't lie," Margret insisted.

"You're lying now."

Margret fell silent. Her armchair had never felt less comfortable than it felt supporting her then, but it supported her when nothing else did. "Do you have a name?" she asked him.

He smiled, with the most self-satisfied smile Margret had ever seen. "You can think of me as a community organizer," he answered her. "You call me Judge."

"This is Saturday," said Margret. "Even if I wanted to do what you say, I can't telephone the aged-care agency on a Saturday. No one will be there."

Her words were true, although there was an emergency contact telephone number she could dial at any time. Judge didn't need to know that.

Judge stared at her, without the aggression of previous stares but more absently, as if he were thinking, before setting his eyes upon her again. "We want you to write a letter to the agency," he told her, "confessing your lies. You will say you don't want to see that American anymore but want Yahnaa again. When she returns, you will like her service and tell the agency you like it. If you ever go back to your lies, then I'll come back here from Michigan, and the rest of us will come back here from where they live, and we will make sure you tell the truth."

"Writing your letter won't do Yahnaa any good," pleaded Margret. "The agency called her other former clients, who confirmed she arranged with those clients to cancel their arrangements with the agency to employ and pay her directly. My letter won't change what they had to say. Yahnaa still won't get her job back."

Judge leant forward, close to Margret's face. "Yahnaa told me who those liars are," he said. "We will visit them and ensure they write to the agency to correct their lies too."

Margret imagined the aged-care agency receiving several unsolicited letters from people saying they had lied about Yahnaa. The agency surely would not believe them, she thought, before realizing it might.

"That's the racism," continued Judge, standing up again, "that Nepalese people suffer in this country."

"Why do you come here if it's all so awful?"

"You want us to come to work for you, but then you discriminate against us."

"I welcomed Yahnaa," pleaded Margret. "I made her tea. I served her food. I gave her every chance."

"She cared for you, but then you thought you could keep money from her and employ an American."

"I..."

Judge raised his hand and pointed finger, motioning her to stop. He rested his finger on his lips. "Shush," he told Margret. "No more lies."

Silence returned, but it was the anxious silence that preceded more threatening words to come. Margret could not recall ever telling a lie. This might be the time she started.

The five young men continued staring down at her from their semicircle confining her to her chair, with Margret looking meekly back up at them from her cushioned cell, until one of the men beside Judge whispered into Judge's ear. They both turned away from Margret.

Their conversation continued, before they both turned back to Margret. As always, Judge was next to speak. "We're going to give you time to write your letter," he told her. "We're going to leave you, before coming back at six o'clock to collect your letter."

Margret breathed more easily. She didn't let the Nepalese see she did, for then they'd know she hadn't been.

Judge smiled. "Because we're so nice," he said, "we'll post your letter for you. We might even deliver it."

Near Margret's home was a blue Postal Service mailbox. She had never visited the aged-care agency offices.

Judge's smile abated, again leaning towards her, his face closer than ever before to hers. "If we come back," he continued, "and you're not here, then you're not going to have much of a home when you do come back. If we come back and see you've brought other people here, thinking they'll protect you, then we won't come into your home, but some future day or night we will. It might be tonight, or tomorrow night. It might not be for another week or another month, but we will come back. I can't tell you what we're going to do, because I don't know what we're going to do, but you're going to end up wishing you'd written your letter, telling the truth about Yahnaa."

Margret sat still. If she had time to cry for help between their pending departure and their return, she wasn't certain that she should.

"Do you understand me?" asked Judge.

Margret nodded. Judge stood so very close to her.

Judge stood upright again. He turned and left the room. The other men followed him into the hallway.

Margret remained in her armchair, listening to their every step departing. The sounds of birds outside suggested her front door remained open, as did the air in the lounge room becoming cooler than it should have been; Margret pulled her cardigan closer to her. Her front door might have remained open since they entered.

The time was after ten o'clock. Margret had eight hours before they would return.

On a table was the telephone. Calling the police would keep her safe at six o'clock. It might not keep her safe thereafter.

She could not give the police any names, except Yahnaa's name. Yahnaa wasn't going to give the police any names, except Margret's. If she'd seen a car from which the young men came then Margret could have described it to the police (although she wasn't very good at identifying types of cars), but she hadn't seen them in a car. Her problems seemed altogether small for America's police.

Quietly, Margret stood up from her armchair. Treading softly, she stepped across the lounge room towards the open hallway door. Before entering the hallway, she stopped and looked around the doorway and along the hallway towards the front door left open. Nobody was there.

Not quite as quietly, Margret stepped along the hallway towards the door, looking through it towards the street for those young men. They had all gone.

Margret's home stood up a small hill from a leafy suburban street of similarly comfortable homes. From her open front door, her street was still and quiet. No car was parked there filled with occupants that she could see. No car drove away.

Margret was again alone, and never more glad to be alone, but her aloneness would not last past six o'clock. She thought of people she might call. Her niece in upstate New York was too far away. Her last friends left alive in Virginia were too old. The aged-care agency that sent her Yahnaa would not consider Margret's problem as its problem; it might become involved when it received so many letters about Yahnaa.

What remained were the people closest to her, best able to look out their windows to see her home and her, best able to take her into their homes. They had something at stake when something threatened their tranquil suburbia.

Retrieving her front door key from inside her home but carrying nothing else, Margret was particularly careful to lock her front door after stepping outside. There, she hesitated, looking around the neighborhood to see that none of the young men who had visited her that morning, or indeed anybody else, was watching her.

Nobody was, unless somebody was watching her from a window of a nearby house. She might be glad if someone there was watching her but, as best as she could see from the doorstep to her home, nobody was.

All the neighbors Margret had known well enough to call her friends had moved away. What remained were those she had seen from her windows but never met, even if she smiled towards them when she saw them and who smiled when they saw her, returning from having checked her mailbox.

Margret tramped from her home down to the sidewalk, along which she proceeded to the nearest driveway adjoining hers. Like Margret's home, that front path and driveway had no gates. Soon, she stood at that front door, upon which she'd often knocked years earlier when her neighbors were her friends, before those neighbors moved away. Margret knocked again.

Soon opening the door in front of her was an ably built young man, although he was really middle aged. He stood smartly dressed for a Saturday, in what was almost a suit. He was also white.

"I am sorry to trouble you," said Margret, "but I live next door, and a group of five young men has just threatened me."

He stepped close to her to look around her to the street. He would have seen no young men. "You better come in," he told her. "My name is Athol Lafferty."

"Margret Wilkie."

After closing the front door behind her, Athol led her into his spacious, brightly furnished lounge room and a chair among several chairs. Sitting in that chair, in a home feeling something of a haven as hers no longer felt, Margret waited. Her house key resting on her lap, she planned what she should say to Athol.

Her host soon brought her a cup of tea to drink and him a glass of water. Athol pulled a chair towards her and sat closely facing her. "You better tell me what's happened," he said.

Margret took a single sip of warm tea, before resting her cup back in the saucer in her hand. She then told Athol the story of her morning.

Athol listened, sometimes nodding, until she finished. "You could still call the police," he told her.

"Near six o'clock," said Margret, "could you please secretly watch the street outside my home? Film any people coming to my home, recording their car and registration plate; I assume you have one of those 'phones that film. When they're inside my home, telephone me; I will give you my number. Tell me what you saw so I can tell them they were filmed, and if anything happens to me or my home today, or any other day, or night, then you will inform the police. I won't reveal to them your name or where you live. They won't even be certain that it's someone looking out from a house, but they'll know the police can identify them and so they must leave."

Athol again nodded, leaving Margret pleased with the plan she had devised. "How will I recognize these men?" he asked.

"They're all Nepalese."

"Oh," said Athol, sitting back in his chair, "I hadn't realized."

"Is that important?"

"There has obviously been some sort of a misunderstanding," Athol assured her. "You should talk with them about their concerns."

"They threatened to ruin my home and harm me," Margret reminded him, leaning forward, "if I don't lie and say that Yahnaa wasn't lazy, that she didn't offer to accept money from me directly to exclude her agency, and that she didn't steal my possessions."

Athol shook his head. "They wouldn't lie," he assured her.

"Immigrants don't understand our customs."

"These ones understand us," answered Margret, "better than we understand ourselves."

Athol smiled. "I am a Christian," he told her. "My wife and our children, they're not here at present, are Christians."

"As am I."

"Christ commands us to love our neighbor."

"Am I not your neighbor?"

"You live next door," Athol told her. "The people of the world are my neighbors."

"The people of the world aren't your neighbors," Margret corrected him. "Nepalese aren't your neighbors. They don't feel neighborly to us."

"They don't have to know they're my neighbors to be my neighbors."

"Don't they?" asked Margret. "Should I send them here?"

Athol smiled. "Please do," he told her.

Margret shook her head. "Only I can sign the letter they demand," she told him. "You were quite willing to help me, when you presumed these men frightening me were Americans?"

"I pray for immigrants," Athol explained. "Every day, I pray that Americans be more generous with them: that we welcome the stranger."

"I did welcome a stranger. I shouldn't have."

"At six o'clock," resumed Athol, "bring those good young men into your home and serve them some tea, as I have served you."

"They're not like me," Margret tried to convince him. "They're not like you."

"Talk with them, listen to what's troubling them: their desires to do a good day's work and be recognized for it; their honesty, and the offence they feel to be accused of dishonesty; their need to be accepted by us. Give them an opportunity to help. You won't be disappointed."

Margret stared at him for much too long a time, before sighing. Having only drunk that initial sip of tea, she offered Athol's cup and saucer back to him. "Thank you for the tea," she said. Collecting her house key from her lap, Margret stood. "I should leave."

Athol walked with her back to the front door, which he opened for her. Again, he smiled at her, with eyes that had come to seem vacuous. "I promise you, Margret," he told her, "you have nothing to fear from immigrants."

"That's what I used to think. I too was wrong." She gave Athol another moment looking at him, without response from him, before speaking again. "You and your family are always welcome in my home," she smiled, "neighbor."

"Bless you," smiled Athol. She left.

To the other side of Margret's home, the house was surrounded by a wall. Gates sealed the driveway, as they hadn't when the previous owners lived there.

Margret stood at the gates, looking for a means of opening them, but couldn't see one. There was no lock between them or bolt into the ground.

Looking around, to the wall at each side of the gates, a small keypad and speaker to one side drew her slowly towards it. Unfamiliar with such security, although aware of it in other places, Margret struggled to read any words or numbers on the keypad without her reading glasses. Her uneasy finger searched for a button to press.

That button she pressed, before quickly pulling back her finger. There she stood, more anxiously than she stood waiting for a door to answer.

"Yes," sounded a voice from the speaker.

Margret jolted back, before slowly edging closer to it. She reached her face and mouth near to the speaker, not knowing what part of the security pad would pick up her voice. "My name is Margret Wilkie," she said. "I live next door. I need to speak with you."

After a moment's hesitation, something clicked, a motor turned, and the gates clunked open. They made Margret visiting her neighbor's home more dramatic than she wanted it to be.

Standing at the front door, watching Margret approach, was another man dressed well for a Saturday. He was younger than her other neighbor and a little overweight around his waist and in his face. "I am Isaac Gaber," he said as she reached him. "Which house is yours?"

Margret pointed towards it. "That one," she said. The gates across Isaac's driveway were already clunking closed behind her.

"My parents aren't home," said Isaac, remaining at his front door.

"May I please sit down?"

Again, he hesitated, before stepping back, admitting Margret into his home. His front door closed behind them, he led her into his darkly furnished, poorly lit home, but only as far as the hallway. He stopped by a chair against a wall, in which Margret sat, her house key in her hand.

Isaac sat in another chair, facing her. "I am going out soon," he said.

Margret repeated the story of her morning she had already said once. She omitted mention of the last time she recited it.

Isaac listened, watching her without expression, until she finished. "What will you do?" he asked.

"Shortly before six o'clock," said Margret, "from your house, could you please secretly film people coming to my home, getting out of their car, or cars? I shall give you my telephone number so you can tell me their car registration plates and I can tell them. I won't let them know who you are or where you live, but they'll know that if anything happens to me or my home, then you will provide the police with your film."

Isaac nodded. "I should be home again before six o'clock," he told her.

Margret smiled, reaching out her hands wanting to touch his, but they sat too far apart. "Thank you, so much," she told him. "My other neighbors say they're Christians, but wouldn't help me."

"I am Jewish."

"I hadn't known."

"How could you have known?"

"You don't wear a…," said Margret, raising her hand a short distance above her head where her fingers fidgeted, "one of those small caps. You don't have a beard."

"I'm not religious."

"My other neighbors, those supposed Christians, wouldn't help me because the young men threatening me are Nepalese."

"Oh," said Isaac, sitting upright. "You can't expect me to defend white people against people of other descent."

"Aren't you white?"

"I'm not white!" snapped Isaac, clenching his fists. "I'm Jewish."

Margret didn't understand, but there were many things she didn't understand. "Would you help me if I was Jewish?" she asked him.

"You didn't help us when we were dying in the camps."

Margret needed time to understand, before slowly remembering. "We fought a war for you," she told him. "We died, saving you."

"We died," said Isaac. "You survived."

Margret dipped her head, seeing only her frail lap and another person's floor. "We're not surviving now," she sighed. "You're punishing me for something that happened somewhere else before you were born, before your parents were born."

"My grandparents were me," said Isaac. "Your grandparents were you."

Still looking down, Margret shook her head. "Unlike you," she told him, "needing to be your grandparents to have lived through World War II, I'm old enough to have lived through that war having been only me. When will it end?"

The ensuing silence was time, hoped Margret, for Isaac to mellow. She remained a poor white woman in distress, at risk of being harmed, or worse, he wasn't taking in.

Margret looked back at Isaac. "If you or your parents had come to my late husband and me wanting help, we would have helped," she told him. "A day ago, if you or your parents had come to me wanting help, although I don't know what help a weakening old woman could be, I would have helped you."

"And now," asked Isaac, "are you saying you wouldn't help me, because I'm Jewish? We have a word for that."

"I'm no longer willing to help people who would refuse to help me," Margret explained. "Is there a word for you not helping me because I'm white?"

Isaac shook his head. "No, there isn't," he answered her. "You can't expect me to defend your prejudice."

"Fearing these five Nepalese young men, quite apart from any more of them they might bring, doesn't make me prejudiced."

"What does it make you?"

Margret continued staring at him. "I have good reason to fear them."

"Prejudiced people all think their fears are justified," said Isaac, "but people get hurt."

"People are already being hurt," said Margret, tears collecting in her eyes. "I will be hurt."

"Prejudice is irrational," insisted Isaac. "It has to be."

"Why must prejudice be irrational?" asked Margret. "Why?"

"Because if prejudice can be rational, then…," Isaac started to say, before hesitating. "You can't know how prejudice feels."

Margret gave him time to explain, and her time to wonder how much she should ask. "What prejudice have you experienced?" she asked him.

"Your prejudice revives my history, scalding me with it."

That history was one Isaac wasn't willing to release. Nor was he willing to release Margret. "I know the feeling of fear," she told him.

"Fear you can forget," replied Isaac. "Fear you can push aside. Go back to your home, lock your doors. Affix more locks if you must. Put bars on your windows and install security alarms. Put walls around your home. Do whatever you have to do, until you no longer feel afraid."

Margret started to ask a question, until she realized she had no need to ask. She looked away from Isaac along the hallway to where she saw a window. Bars covered it.

She looked up to the cornices and corners of the ceiling. A security sensor pointed down and along the hallway.

Margret looked back to the front door, which a platoon of locks and bolts sealed. On the wall beside the door was a small keypad and speaker like the one beside the gates from the street, but also a second panel and large screen from which were visible four images from outside. Before opening the gates across the driveway, Isaac would have seen Margret waiting outside. "Are you still afraid, Isaac?" she asked, turning back towards him.

Isaac sat staring at her, before finally speaking. "I think you should leave now," he said. "I will tell my parents what you've told me about your visitors."

"They might read about it in the newspaper."

"They're more likely to read about Nepalese suffering job discrimination, or being harassed by police."

Without any joy in doing so, Margret laughed. "That's true," she said, standing up.

Her house key still in her hand, Margret shuffled ahead of Isaac to his front door. She started trying to open it, but there were too many locks and bolts for her to manage. Isaac stepped around her and, with the skill that came from experience, opened the door for her.

Outside the door, Margret stopped. She looked up, and saw a camera looking down.

"I want people to see that," said Isaac. "I want them seeing the security alarm high up on the side of the house." Margret hadn't noticed it.

She trudged back down the driveway to the gates still closed. As Margret neared them, they opened. When she had passed through them, they closed again, when she saw Isaac still watching her from his home. If he had watched her to be certain that she was leaving, he could be satisfied she had gone.

Isaac stepped back into his home. Margret would not return.

Across the street were several houses facing hers. Margret could have knocked upon their doors looking for more people she didn't know, but she'd had enough of strangers telling her she was alone. She trekked back to her home.

Opening Margret's front door was a single lock. The lock that once had been enough in homes across America, and might even have been too much security when neighbors were friends, no longer was, but no number of locks would be enough anymore.

The time was not yet noon. Margret had more than six hours before the Nepalese would return, expecting her to give them the letter they would deliver to the aged-care agency.

Having collected her reading glasses from beside her armchair in the lounge room, Margret climbed back upstairs to her study she'd often entered when she worked but rarely entered anymore. Much as the Nepalese expected her to do, she sat at her desk, where she pushed aside a handful of bank statements and the like.

Rarely did she write or receive anything personal in her mail anymore. There were only banking matters and accounts to be paid.

From a drawer, Margret removed some writing paper. She removed an envelope and a postage stamp she affixed to the envelope. She put on her reading glasses.

Lying had never come easily to Margret; she had grown up at a time lying did not come easily to any ordinary American. She was too old to change. Margret might have also been too old to care about the consequences of not telling the truth, in the strange and lonely new America.

Taking a fountain pen she wasn't certain still provided ink until it did, Margret began writing everything that had happened to her since Yahnaa arrived at her home two weeks earlier. She began writing a long letter to the only person left alive she felt she could: her niece in upstate New York.

12 PUBLISHING

Through the nineteenth and early twentieth centuries, vulgarity upset American publishers and readers, although language they found vulgar was poetic purity aside the cussing, swearing, and blasphemy that would later become stock American writing. Two decades into the twenty-first century, it seemed that no word remained offensive, however shocking it might once have been.

Conversely, other words previously commonplace had become grossly offensive to American sensibilities. They incited reactions from publishers and readers far more hysterical than the reactions mere words elicited from their forebears.

Among the newly offensive words were any connoting race; racial language had become offensive whenever race was offensive. As much as Americans hated racism, they hated words connoting racism. Not even racists took on the aggravation of using such words, when strangers could hear. It wasn't worth the trouble.

The people who'd never think of using racial language, or any other offensive language, included Calvin Hart and Nate Pilben. They'd been friends since their time at school together in upstate New York, best man at each other's weddings, and godfather to the other's children. With Nate's hair receding sooner than Calvin's hair, they survived their New York City careers well enough to reach fifty-seven years of age.

Throughout their working lives, they'd been a little envious of each other's vocations, as they both often liked to say, until Calvin decided he'd earned enough money from corporate law to retire. He then embarked upon his passion common to many lawyers, if not so common in corporations: literature.

Nate had forged his career in publishing, which he often complained to Calvin would never provide him with the money to retire without leaving New York, and he and his wife would never leave New York. In spite of his inadequate financial reward, some of the authors and books that later became household names first entered Calvin's head because Nate enthused about them to him, although there seemed at least as many authors and books that Nate lauded, even time and again, that Calvin never heard or read mentioned by anyone else.

In spite of applicable laws, Calvin's age would have excluded him from most jobs in New York, at least the sorts of jobs people like he and Nate wanted, but what remained Nate's lifetime career became Calvin's opening into something he insisted was not a new career. Calvin edited manuscripts for Nate's publishing house in his family home at the end of a commuter train journey, where the woods were a world away from busy skyscrapers and crowds. Editing wasn't a job because Calvin would have done edited for free, although Nate insisted upon paying him what his publishing house paid other editors.

Sometimes, Nate gave manuscripts to Calvin or Calvin returned manuscripts to him at one of their homes or over restaurant meals, with as much sociable conversation as any about the manuscripts. Other times, manuscripts were couriered to or from Calvin's home with barely a word spoken between them, except to confirm that Calvin had the time to edit: that he wasn't about to embark upon another short vacation with his wife or other voluntary activity commanding his time.

When Calvin had another reason to travel into Manhattan, or was simply in the mood to return more leisurely than he could while working, he boarded the train back there. With him, he carried his new soft brown leather briefcase, which felt altogether more relaxed than the formal black leather briefcase he'd carried in his corporate career. Sometimes, his new briefcase carried manuscripts he'd edited to return to Nate. Other times, it would collect more manuscripts from Nate for him to edit. Often, it did both.

Walking to Nate's offices, on the thirtieth floor of a forty-story building along the Avenue of the Americas, could feel just a little like Calvin was again a corporate lawyer, but for that brown leather briefcase and the clothes he wore, freed from the dictates of his career. His turtleneck sweaters, of wool in winter and silk in summer, and blazers would have been too casual for a corporate lawyer to wear, but were acceptable, if not a little formal, for an editor entering a publishing house. He arrived at Nate's offices late of a weekday morning, if in the morning at all, because neither man still started early any morning.

One late Thursday morning, ready to bring home two manuscripts to edit, Calvin's briefcase would have been empty, without a manuscript to return edited that day, but for his surprise for Nate. It was a manuscript that he'd not only edited, several times over (if revision was akin to editing an author's own work), but one he'd written.

After Calvin entered Nate's private office, Nate closed the door behind them. Nate didn't normally close the door to give Calvin manuscripts to edit.

On Nate's round glass table lay two manuscripts. Calvin stood his briefcase on the table beside them.

While everything else in Nate's offices was contemporary, futuristic even, in a corner of Nate's office stood a gumball machine. Calvin's offices had never housed anything so frivolous, but he helped himself to a gumball each time he arrived there; visiting Nate's office were the only times Calvin still ate gumballs.

Standing together at the table, Calvin chewing his gumball, Nate picked up a manuscript. "This is the Mississippi manuscript I mentioned on the telephone," said Nate. A retired schoolteacher in Mississippi had written a novel in homage to American novelist Mark Twain. Like Twain's most famous novels, familiar to American readers for generations, this new novel was set in the nineteenth century along the Mississippi River.

Nate opened the manuscript to an early page and, as if unwilling to say them aloud, pointed Calvin's attention to two words Twain had also used in his books, as originally written and published. (Only Calvin was with Nate in his office and the door was closed, so Nate can't have feared someone overhearing him if he spoke those words.) Employing the vernacular common among poor people in the place and time described, the manuscript characters abbreviated mention of Indians and Negroes to something colloquial.

"You'll want to change those words," said Nate, in his words of preparation that he didn't give Calvin for every manuscript Calvin would edit, but he gave for this one.

"Why?"

"Have you seen those words in print?" asked Nate. "I haven't, and I've seen a lot of words in print. I've never heard them spoken."

Calvin stepped back, leaving Nate holding his manuscript. "The writer's describing people who used them," said Calvin. "Who are we to say otherwise?"

"We're publishers."

"Do we ever ask what normal people think?"

"We are normal people," insisted Nate. "Weren't you the great advocate of diversity when you worked, worrying about what everyone said?"

Still chewing his gumball, Calvin rested in a black cushioned chair, where he often rested when he visited Nate's office. "I've been thinking a lot about truth lately," said Calvin, "now that I'm not thinking about law and business all the time."

Nate returned the manuscript to the table. "This isn't about truth, Calvin. It's about publishing."

"It's about business, Nate. I was in business long enough to recognize it."

"So you understand my point of view," said Nate, sitting in a cushioned chair facing him. "I've never heard you use those words you're trying to save from expurgation."

"I'm not offended to read words I don't use. I let authors tell me the words their characters use; they know those characters before I do."

Calvin's visits to Nate's office normally turned to conversations more sociable than this one, although few of them as earnest. "This publishing house is built upon us knowing what readers want," said Nate. "Never hearing racial language today, Americans don't want to read of it from olden days."

"Those words reflect life of old," persisted Calvin. "They weren't insults, not then. They were abbreviations, you know that. They were slang."

"Racial abbreviations are racist," insisted Nate. "Insert their names. Call them people."

"That's boring."

"Call them indigenous or Native Americans and African Americans."

"Those terms didn't exist, or barely existed, before the 1960s."

"Call them slaves," continued Nate.

"They mightn't have been slaves."

"Today's readers think they were. Who are we to say otherwise?"

"We're people who know they weren't slaves," answered Calvin, chewing his gum, "unless this manuscript says they were."

"How often does a book need to allude to somebody's race?"

"The author thought these characters did."

Nate smiled. "When I publish a book," he declared, "I am the author."

"You didn't like to see publishers corrupt Mark Twain's books with words he didn't choose," Calvin reminded him, "that mean so much less."

"America's moved on since I said that. I'd correct the classics now if I needed to, but this book isn't a classic. It's a book that I think can sell enough copies to be worthwhile to people who read Twain, by a retired Mississippi schoolteacher I think has more books in him, but right now it means nothing to anyone but him and whatever hicks have told him he can write. If he asks, I'll tell him we're not publishing his virgin words without the changes I require. He'll agree, because otherwise nobody's going to publish them and nobody's going to read them."

"Not all publishers are in New York," countered Calvin.

"The important publishers are in New York."

"You think the only important people are in New York. I understand that, I thought the same in my Manhattan office."

"Sometimes," said Nate, "I think I preferred you in your Manhattan office."

The gum Calvin chewed had become tasteless. "We never used to be paranoid about race," he lamented.

"Editors have to be paranoid about race. I have to be paranoid."

"I have to be honest."

"I don't want honest books, Calvin. I want books people buy."

"Don't readers want honesty, Nate?"

"Readers want affirmation of what they already believe. Re-engage them with reality and they'll hate you for it."

Resigned to not reading that manuscript but conscious of the cue it gave him, Calvin rose from his chair. He returned to the gumball machine, where he took a paper napkin from the small pile of napkins. Calvin removed the tasteless gum from his mouth, wrapped it in the napkin, and dropped it in the wastebasket already filling with napkins. "I've written a manuscript," he said.

"Everybody has."

"Can you read it?" asked Calvin, turning back to him. "The only words in it are those I'd use in conversation."

"For you, I'll read the opening line. I'll decide then whether to continue. With every line I read, I'll decide whether to continue. You're better off me doing that than trying to be generous with my time, when other readers aren't so generous."

Calvin returned to the glass table. "Is there a point at which you keep reading even if you didn't like the line you read?" he asked.

"Isn't there for you, unless you're being paid to read?"

Calvin removed from his briefcase a manuscript he placed on the table. "There used to be."

Nate stood beside him. "The Populist Manifesto," said Nate, reading the title page. "You have come a long way."

From the two manuscripts Nate had offered him, Calvin took the second: the one to which Nate hadn't introduced him. He slipped it into his briefcase.

"Take the Mississippi manuscript," said Nate. "If I don't like what you do with it, I won't pay you. I'll pay an editor who'll do with this baby what I want her to do with it."

Calvin also slipped that manuscript into his briefcase. He fastened it closed.

Nate took Calvin's manuscript from the table. "I better hide this," he said, carrying it across his office and opening a drawer to his desk. "You worry me when you talk about truth, honesty, and race," he said, putting the manuscript into his drawer, "then give your book a title about populism."

"You don't mind manifesto?"

"I like manifesto," said Nate, closing his desk drawer. "A hundred years ago, a manifesto terrified people, but not now."

With Calvin carrying his brown briefcase and Nate's two manuscripts inside, they walked together to Nate's office door. Nate opened his door, for them to see an aging colleague of Nate stumbling over himself, looking worse than his stylish canary yellow suit should have made him. "I've had the most God-awful morning," the man complained to Nate. "Thank God, I made it." He stumbled out of sight.

Calvin looked at Nate. "Does he believe in God?" asked Calvin. "He mentioned Him twice."

"It's just a word."

"It's not a word we expunge from books."

Nate smiled. "We only expunge mention of God if anyone

means it."

"Blasphemy we leave in books," remarked Calvin. "Books and films are filled with characters swearing and uttering profanities far more than real people do, but would we cull those words because readers found them offensive?"

"Are you turning Godly on me now, Calvin?"

"Can't you see the contrast with us purging words that real people used at the time books describe?"

"Think of it as our modern-day obscenity law, Calvin. What was obscene, no longer is. What was not obscene, now is."

Calvin shook his head. "Not only are past obscenities no longer obscene," he remarked, "they're practically mandatory."

Nate laughed. "Read old editions then, my friend," he said, "if you can find them."

Calvin smiled. "I do," he said, departing.

Neither man mentioned manuscripts when Calvin and Nate arranged their next time together, two weeks later. It would again be dinner in the 21 Club restaurant, along West 52nd Street.

Decades of dining there, with his wife, Nate, and other friends and businesspeople, had cost Calvin the sense of cozy elegance he must have felt when first he entered the 21 Club, as it had of all the fine restaurants at which he ate. Instead, there was comfortable familiarity, which he and Nate wanted more than they wanted anything new in their eating places. Whosever turn it was to pay didn't matter, as they'd both gladly pay when the time to pay arose.

Calvin arrived with his brown leather briefcase, hanging loosely from his hand. Nate arrived carrying a black leather briefcase, unusually, close to his side.

The maître d' greeted them. "May I take those for you, gentlemen?" he asked.

Calvin and Nate replied simultaneously. "In a moment," said Calvin.

"In a few minutes," said Nate.

Thus Calvin and Nate sat at their small table for two, to which the maître d' directed them. Calvin stood his briefcase on the floor beside his chair; there was no risk of theft in the 21 Club. Nate stood his briefcase on the floor beside him, but continued holding it.

The maître d' left them with their menus on the table, awaiting their attention. Their drinks would soon arrive.

Calvin reached down beside his chair and opened his briefcase. He removed from it a white envelope he placed on the table. "This is the Mississippi manuscript," he told Nate. "I liked it."

"Will I be paying you for the edit?" asked Nate, his free hand taking the envelope.

Calvin smiled. "Another editor probably needs the money."

Nate's other hand still held his briefcase. He reached down towards it, taking with him the white envelope out of Calvin's sight. "It might be better if I don't look at this too soon," he remarked.

Nate brought up in its place a thick yellow envelope, he lay on the table. The envelope was unmarked, but sealed. Calvin didn't need an inscription to know it contained his manuscript.

"You should have stayed in your career," said Nate. "You should have confined yourself to editing other people's manuscripts."

Nate pushed the envelope across the cloth towards Calvin, who took it in his hand. He placed it in his briefcase, he then closed.

"You should lock that," said Nate.

The maître d' again appeared at their table. "May I take those now?" he asked them.

"Thank you," answered Calvin, offering his briefcase purposefully unlocked. He'd have liked nothing more than to have a stranger take and read his manuscript.

Nate offered the maître d' his briefcase. It was probably locked.

The maître d' left them alone, as alone as they could be in a crowded restaurant; 21 Club was always crowded. Calvin sipped from the glass of cold water in front of him. A waiter brought Calvin a glass of beer. He also brought a bottle of wine, from which he poured Nate a glass before leaving.

Nate was next to speak. "I read all your manuscript," he said.

"Shouldn't that mean you liked it?"

"I read it for the same reason that people stare at train wrecks: drawn by the disaster, wishing I wasn't."

"We used to be the greatest train on earth," responded Calvin, "or carriages in the greatest train on earth: coach class when we started, becoming first class. Don't you remember how good our lives were when we were young, Nate, how nice this city was, before everybody came?"

Nate shook his head. "Readers don't like those sorts of thoughts," he said. "People won't buy books I publish if I think like that. Besides, I'd be drummed out of the industry before I published anything again."

"Don't you want to save the train, Nate?"

"The train feels fine to me."

"When all you do is look out the window, all you see is the view."

Nate laughed. He wasn't supposed to. "I don't publish books by authors wanting readers to hate them, and so me," he said. "Your ideas are revolutionary."

"This country formed in revolution. We might need another revolution to save her."

Nate shook his head. "You've had way too much time to think since you stopped working," he said. "Why can't you be content with vacations, restaurants, and television, like other retirees? Take a wine appreciation course or learn to play bridge. Vote Republican, maybe Libertarian, and talk about your aching bones, skin rashes, and indigestion."

"I don't want to lie on my deathbed thinking all I've done with my late life is play cards, with people who are dead."

"They won't have minded."

"I'd mind, Nate."

"Didn't you always want to visit Lima?"

Calvin smiled. "I haven't done everything I've wanted to do in my life," he said, "but if I really wanted to do something, I would. What I've realized is that those things I haven't done aren't important, but our people are important. There's conflict, thinly veiled or not, wherever different races live together, which white people now try to soothe by appeasing other races, from our secret swanky offices like those I used to occupy. What do you think will happen if we become a minority in this country, Nate?"

"There is nothing to think about, Calvin."

"What if there is something to think about, Nate?"

A waitress appeared beside them. "We should order our meals," said Nate.

They ordered. The waitress left, taking away their menus.

"My advice, my friend," said Nate, as they both pulled apart their bread rolls, "is that you burn your book in your fireplace, either one of your fireplaces, out there in the woods where you live. Burn it page by page so you can be certain every word is destroyed. Then pound the ashes into a pulp so no one reconstructs them.

Then drop the pulp into an acid bath."

Nate spread butter on his bread. Calvin sat listening.

"When you're done," continued Nate, "delete every draft and document from your computer and the cloud. Smash your disk drive with a mallet, douse it with more acid, and bury it where not even archaeologists will find it."

Nate brought his buttered bread near his mouth. Calvin's broken bread remained on his plate.

"If anybody asks," said Nate, about to eat, "I'll say I read a lot of manuscripts and can't recall them all. You say you write a lot and can't recall every word, but you'd never write a manuscript like that. You believe diversity is America's greatest strength and all that; you know the lyrics. Why, you know it's prejudice causing problems, if there really are any problems. Without discrimination, we're all dandy." Nate placed his bread in his mouth.

"Do you know what's happening in the world?" asked Calvin.

Nate finished his mouthful. "I know what's happening in the books people read and the movies and television they watch," he answered. "I know what publishers and producers say is happening."

"Were Mark Twain alive today," said Calvin, buttering his bread, "he might write a manuscript like mine, with more colorful language than I've employed."

Interrupting them was a man's voice above and beside them. "Nate, dear," he said.

Chewing on his bread, Calvin looked up to see standing by Nate a man wearing a black felt hat, black suit, and holding a small black cane like it was a wand. "Pleasing two or three writers," the man told Nate, still sitting, "and I exhaust my day at a writers' conference in Savannah. Savannah, huh: they're all Gothic in Savannah."

Said the minor character from allegorical fiction, thought Calvin, as Nate looked back at Calvin. "Efrem is in publishing," Nate introduced him.

Efrem continued addressing Nate. "They all think they know America because they know their neighbors, but have you met their neighbors?" Efrem blurted out a noise like a horse clearing its nostrils, shaking his head as might a horse. "Oh, to be home again: New York, where I don't have to know my neighbors to know my neighbors."

"Calvin wants to be a writer," Nate told him, presumably as a favor to Calvin.

Efrem reached down and placed his hand on Calvin's arm. "Don't you be like those amateurs in Savannah," said Efrem. "Don't give us your great American novel." Efrem tossed back his head, taking back his hand from Calvin. "Give us what's already on the *New York Times* bestseller list. Give us what people already read. If people don't read, give us what they buy."

Calvin prepared to thank him for his advice, but Efrem quickly looked back at Nate. Whatever motivated Efrem, it wasn't gratitude.

"Nate, dear," said Efrem. "Are we seeing you at the Goldsteins Sunday night?"

"We wouldn't miss it."

"Super," beamed Efrem, who then glanced at Calvin. "Bye-ee," he smiled, with a wave of his wand, before gliding away.

Nate looked back at Calvin. "What do you think someone like Efrem Meister, or the Goldsteins, would think of your manuscript?" asked Nate.

Calvin looked across the restaurant at Efrem, settling into a table of people like him. All Calvin knew of the Goldsteins was their name, but their name revealed a lot. "I know that we'll appease them," said Calvin, looking back at Nate.

"Efrem gives good advice. If you want to get published, write what everyone else writes, but make it superficially different enough for readers not to notice. Throw in some language your mother never heard and pornography your father couldn't bear and I'll publish it or find a publisher who will, but don't offend their sensibilities around race or you'll be stuck among the scrap, literally speaking."

Calvin shook his head. "I don't want to write books without stories," he said, "about self-absorbed people and their private emotional journeys." Calvin took another piece of bread in his hand. "I want to write stories that make readers think, even if they're as slow to contemplate as I was."

"Americans don't want to think. They want to feel."

"I want them to think and feel."

"Save the thinking for mystery novels," said Nate. "Write against racism."

Calvin laughed. "Everybody does," he replied, before eating the bread from his hand.

"Write about immigrants overcoming adversity to contribute to multicultural America," Nate elaborated. "Heck, you could write any old gibberish, but make the racists look bad and immigrant America beautiful, and they'll shower you with praise. White people love those books, as do publishers, schoolteachers, and award givers. They'll love you for yours, writing reviews exhorting your brilliance and talent, without having read it."

Calvin laughed, knowing he shouldn't. "Libraries and bookstores are crammed with that fiction," he replied. "I'd rather learn to play bridge than write more."

Nate drank more of his wine. "Did you think like this while you worked, Calvin?" he asked.

"I've matured since then."

"It's not the sort of maturing you want to do."

"I could self-publish," persisted Calvin, "picking a publisher name that means something only to me, selling my writing anyway I can."

"Make your manuscript a poem," suggested Nate. "Nobody reads poetry, and you better hope nobody reads yours."

Calvin smiled. "I'll save my poetry for another manuscript nobody reads."

"You've got friends you could lose if they learn what you write."

"Am I losing you, Nate?"

"Not if I can help it, but I might not be able to help it. I haven't earned the money you've earned to cease earning."

Calvin smiled. "What I have, you have."

"You've got a family, Calvin: a loving wife and the many children I wish I had. Don't take on the aggravation your family doesn't need and you can't afford."

"I can afford it, Nate. Aren't children the reason to take on the aggravation? They've got more at stake than we have. They give us our stakes."

"How will it help your children to make their father a social leper, their mother a social widow? Don't talk with your children the way you write. If you want them to get ahead, or even to survive, in America today, teach them to lie."

Calvin laughed. "They might be the only people who read my writing," he admitted, "someday they're old enough to care and I'm too old to speak, or dead, but I'm not the only person to feel as I feel, to think as I think."

"You're the only person I know who admits it."

Calvin looked around the restaurant: at the patrons and, possibly unfairly, the staff. Their pride could seem pretentious, for the feelings hidden there. It was the same pride and pretention he'd felt through his company career.

"Publishers like genres," said Nate, drawing Calvin's attention back to him. "They'll categorize your writing with others they hate in a genre we'll call Fascist literature, because everything they hate they call Fascist."

Calvin had known as much when he'd first typed words that made his manuscript worthwhile. He drank another mouthful of beer.

"People stumbling across your book will write scathing reviews without reading it because they hate your politics," warned Nate. "They'll feel mightily pleased with themselves for pushing readers away from your politics by pushing them away from your book. They won't care how they do it. People will fight you."

"They've been fighting populism since we stopped defending it."

"If your book amounts to anything, they'll find a means to kill it. You'll know you're somebody when powerful people ban you."

"What of the First Amendment?" asked Calvin. "The Supreme Court counts more than Congress and companies."

"Who'll take your case there?" asked Nate. "Who'll be seen to back you, and cop the flak you'd have copped if Congress or companies cared enough to intervene? There'll be votes and money in stopping you but only punishment for backing you. They're not going to let you divide this country…"

"They've divided this country," interjected Calvin. "Now, they're destroying it, as they're destroying other countries they've infested with their ideas."

Nate shook his head. "Are you really the man I've known all my life?" he asked.

Calvin smiled. "I should tell you what's happening with America," he said. Calvin proceeded to tell Nate about his niece who'd applied for accountancy jobs in Delaware and been offered interviews because firms thought she was Chinese, but lost those interviews when they leant she wasn't.

Nate asked occasional questions he must have thought would explain the people Calvin described. None of Calvin's answers, such as they were, pointed to anything profound.

Calvin went onto to speak of a nephew who organized a free Christmas gift stall at his Massachusetts church. The nephew became tired of an unappreciative Chechen family taking everything.

A waitress served Calvin and Nate their meals, including a bowl of steaming vegetables. Silently, Calvin surveyed the food, while the waitress ground them some pepper, sprinkled it on their meals, and left.

While they ate, Calvin talked of his cousin in Washington State adopting a Native American baby, discovering race meant more to the growing boy than it meant to her. He spoke of a second cousin in Louisiana, who welcomed his son's black girlfriend, until she expected his son to abandon his whiteness his family had never before appreciated.

Calvin talked while they ate and after they'd finished eating. Representing parents on a panel hiring a schoolteacher in New Jersey, his wife's cousin presumed the candidates' capacity to teach English was important, and that their race was not. No less naïve was his wife's niece teaching school in Maryland, trusting the school had reason to be proud of its racial diversity.

A waitress removed Calvin and Nate's empty plates. Unusually, they ordered desserts, to keep their conversation going.

Awaiting their desserts and while they ate them, Calvin talked of his wife's second cousin suspending all his political donations after his son's experience as an intern to a Congressman who'd long supported immigration, but who realized that changing demographics within his district would cost him his seat. Calvin incorporated his son's research there in *The Populist Manifesto*.

A waitress removed their empty dessert plates. Nate ordered coffee.

Calvin remained with his beer, telling Nate of his wife's late aunt in Virginia, whose Nepalese caregiver refused to give her any care. Her response brought the wrath of other Nepalese upon her, but her Christian and Jewish neighbors refused, for different reasons, to defend her from immigrants.

While Calvin talked, Nate drank his coffee. As Nate finished, Calvin had exhausted the people on point he knew well enough to describe.

"Did you invent those people?" asked Nate.

"Did Harper Lee invent Atticus Finch?"

Nate took a moment to consider that answer, before resuming. "Make their stories your book," he suggested. "People who read books are going to want to hate them: not just hate them, but want to hate them, enjoy hating them. People who don't read books but learn of them will want to hit them."

"Those people I described never hit anyone."

Nate declined the waitress' offer of more coffee. He returned to the last of his wine. "You better give yourself a nom de plume," resumed Nate. "The only person they'll hate more than the people in your book is you for mentioning them."

"Can I mention you?"

"Conceal my identity, but make sure you quote my nom de guerre telling you to destroy your manuscript."

"I wouldn't omit it."

The time was Nate's to drink the last wine in his glass, swilling those last drops down. "You're not going to destroy your manuscript, are you Calvin?"

Calvin smiled, as he drank the last beer in his glass, no quicker with his final mouthful than with any other. He pushed his chair back, preparing to stand, as Nate did the same. "I can't be quiet," said Calvin. "The truth is important. Our future is more important than my little life today."

ABOUT THE AUTHOR

Simon Lennon has lived, worked, and travelled throughout America, Europe, Australasia, Asia, and the South Pacific. He is married with six children. He is the author of the following books.

Short Story Collections
Gender in America
Discovering Race

Novels
The King of a Vacant City
Swansong of a Childless People
A Young Man's Tale
The Insubordinate
Mahmood and Mrs. Wynworth

Non-Fiction
Western Individualism
The End of Natural Selection
The Need for Nations
People's Identity
Of Whom We're Born
Biological Us
A Land to Belong
The Failure of Multiculturalism
Reclaiming Western Cultures
Christendom Lost
Aiding Islam